'See you then. Goodnight.'
    And then he was gone, just gone, vanished into
the

tob

aga

a h

Da

a g

gli

ve

dri

the

mi

the
tarot
reader's
DAUGHTER

helen**DUNWOODIE**

Corgi Books

THE TAROT READER'S DAUGHTER
A CORGI BOOK 978 0 552 55190 8 (from January 2007)
0 552 55190 2

Published in Great Britain by Corgi Books,
an imprint of Random House Children's Books

This edition published 2006

1 3 5 7 9 10 8 6 4 2

Papers used by Random House Children s Books are natural,
recyclable products made from wood grown in sustainable forests.
The manufacturing processes conform to the environmental
regulations of the country of origin.

Set in 11/16pt Palatino by
Falcon Oast Graphic Art Ltd.

Corgi Books are published by Random House Children's Books,
61–63 Uxbridge Road, London W5 5SA,
a division of The Random House Group Ltd,
in Australia by Random House Australia (Pty) Ltd,
20 Alfred Street, Milsons Point, Sydney, NSW 2061, Australia,
in New Zealand by Random House New Zealand Ltd,
18 Poland Road, Glenfield, Auckland 10, New Zealand,
and in South Africa by Random House (Pty) Ltd,
Isle of Houghton, Corner of Boundary Road & Carse O'Gowrie,
Houghton 2198, South Africa

THE RANDOM HOUSE GROUP Limited Reg. No. 954009
www.**kids**at**random**house.co.uk

A CIP catalogue record for this book is available from the
British Library.

Printed and bound in Great Britain by
Bookmarque Ltd, Croydon, Surrey

With thanks to the Scottish Arts Council;
the Sanctuary Café, Hove, and Florentin's,
Stockbridge; and to the gallus lassies
of Random House

This book is for everyone who's ever
chummed me for a coffee

CHAPTER one

The very first time I saw Andy Byron, I was wandering about in the autumnal woods below my new home and brooding over my lonely fate, so when I realized that I wasn't actually alone, I felt cheated. What was this boy doing, cluttering up the picturesque scene?

There he stood on the wooden bridge at the foot of the hill, leaning on the rail at a shapely angle and completely blocking the wooden causeway.

Of course, I didn't *have* to cross the river. I could go back to the new house in time for Mum's return from the shops, but I wasn't going to let some lad prevent me from exploring my new surroundings.

So I strode down the hill and onto the bridge. He barely looked at me, just hitched himself up enough for me to sidle past. I stamped on, my tatty old trainers slapping on the boards, and then swung right, as though I knew where I was going.

In fact, there was a path alongside the river, probably flocked with joggers and cyclists at weekends, but completely empty on a sunny weekday morning like this one. Nobody for miles around except for me and the boy on the bridge. And anyway, what was he doing here? I had the day off school in order to help Mum with the move, but what was his excuse? Despite myself, I slowed down as the path meandered through a grove of what even I recognized as birch trees, and glanced back. And precisely as I did so, he looked up and our eyes met. I was so furious with myself that I turned sharply away, but even before I'd turned, he had dropped his gaze back to the water.

So I wasn't worth looking at, was I?

I didn't know which made me angrier, his looking or his not looking. I *was* wearing my oldest jeans and T-shirt, and my hair was just shoved up into a clip, so I could hardly blame him. But the incident brought back the bad temper against which I'd been struggling all day. I'd just been telling myself that I didn't *really* mind moving out of Edinburgh, and that all this red and gold nature stuff was actually quite pretty, and the very first person I meet is this loathsome boy!

I sat down on a big stone and stared gloomily into the river. It was just fate that I'd been dragged away from all my friends and dumped here at the end of the bus route. I couldn't even blame Mum and Dad. I leaned my head on my hands in order to mope more effectively, but as I did so, I caught sight of my watch and sprang to my feet. Midday! Mum would be back by now with her load of scrubbing brushes and Mr Muscle cleaning products and I hadn't finished washing out the kitchen cupboards.

I began to trot back along the path. I'd have to go past the boy again, and this time he'd know I'd been interested enough to look back at him. However, when I reached the bridge he was gone, nothing left of him but a couple of fagends. What a poser, smoking himself to death in the fresh air.

Yet I had to admit that the pose had been effective. Longish black hair, battered old leather jacket, washed-out jeans. I wondered if he lived around here. If he did, I was bound to see him again – not that I cared, of course. He looked too much like the sort of boy who had a very high opinion of his own charms.

By now I'd reached the steep bit of the path so I concentrated on weaving my way around thickets of gorse and bramble and under various trees. I just hoped that, come summer, none of the McBride family developed hay fever. That would really be ironic.

Then the path levelled out behind the gardens bordering our new home. I panted my way to the end of the row and through the back gate. Too late. There was the car drawn up beside the little brick dolls' house, and Mum unloading the boot. She straightened up when she saw me coming.

'Rosa*leen*, I can't leave you to do anything! Did you finish the cupboards?'

'More or less.'

'More or less? What sort of answer's that? You know I want to do as much as I can today.'

'Sorry, Mum, I'd run out of Flash. And I wanted to see what it was like down by the river.'

Normally, Mum would've made some sort of 'Och, away with you' remark, but today she said, 'Now you're here, take this box inside. And don't go dashing off again. There's work to be done.'

Mum had been definitely ratty ever since the three fatal things had happened: traffic, re-routed from the city centre, had begun to pour past our old flat; the piece of wasteland opposite had become a dusty building site; and my little brother, Nairn, had had his first serious asthma attack.

Nairn has always been a bit wheezy, but once he'd actually been issued with an inhaler, Mum and Dad sprang into action and began househunting. They'd been making vague noises for years about moving out of town, but as they both like city life – especially Dad, who grew up on a small farm – I'd never taken them seriously.

'How about a cup of coffee first?' I suggested, in the hope of calming Mum down.

'Not yet – the van might be here any minute.'

Mum and I had come on ahead to clean, as the nice young couple from whom we'd bought the house had left it surprisingly dirty.

'I wonder if this is a good day to move according to the stars?' I said, hauling a box out of the boot. 'I meant to look at my horoscope this morning, but I forgot.'

'Honestly, Rosa, that stuff's nothing but blethers,' snapped Mum. She has no time for astrology or any of what she calls 'New Age palaver'. 'Now let's take these things into the house. We can't unpack the china unless we've got clean cupboards to put it into,' she said, and seized an enormous box of cleaning products and whooshed off with it as though she were some mythic female warrior instead of a petite hairdresser. I picked up the remaining box and followed her, deciding not to mention that the reason we were running late was because she'd packed the wrong boxes in the first place. What she'd thought was cleaning stuff had turned out to be all the things that had mysteriously gathered themselves on top of her wardrobe for the past umpteen years. So she'd made an emergency dash to the nearest shopping centre, while I'd been left cleaning as best I could with an old rag and some dregs of Flash abandoned by the previous owners.

'Now, you line the cupboards you've washed out and then start on the surfaces, and I'll get in here under the sink.' And Mum's silky red ponytail, only slightly henna-enhanced, disappeared into the cupboard.

Mum and I do look a bit alike, although, while she's a redhead, I've inherited Dad's curly dark hair and what I think is an unfashionably healthy milkmaid complexion.

Anyway, we both worked flat out for an hour, which at least took my mind off the encounter on the bridge, and by the time we'd finished, the kitchen looked like the 'after' bit of a TV ad. Only then did Mum allow us to let up for a coffee, although she still kept running to the window to see if the van was coming.

To keep out of her way, I took the boxes of wardrobe stuff upstairs and dumped them in a corner. One was full of Mum's childhood Highland dancing trophies, which she won't put on display, no matter how much we nag her, but the other seemed to contain nothing but rubbish. An old pair of crimson stilettos, a paper bag of dusty embroidery thread – why were we carting all this stuff from one place to another? I sat down on the floor and began to sort through the junk. Perhaps I could persuade Mum to part with some of it? These terrible wooly hats, for instance, relics of Dad's hiking days?

And then, as I dug into the box, my fingers met something luxuriously soft. Puzzled, I pulled it out and found myself holding a blue velvet drawstring bag with a squarish object inside. I turned it over in my hands, digging my fingernails into the dense, almost furry material. There was a line of embroidery around the top, a row of little suns and moons and stars, decorated with sequins. I told myself sensibly that it wouldn't hold anything exciting, just broken jewellery or dry make-up. But I was rejecting these thoughts even as I lined them up. I just knew that this carefully decorated bag must contain something special. I knew because my fingers were tingling, and the velvet, despite having been hidden for so long, was mysteriously warm and welcoming to the touch. The bag positively wanted me to open it. I eased the drawn edges apart, the cord ran smoothly back through the hem and something tumbled out onto my lap: a package wrapped in a purple silk scarf.

Carefully, I unfolded the crumpled material – and found myself holding a pack of limp, dog-eared cards. But these weren't normal playing cards. They were too big, and each card bore a brightly coloured picture. And the oddest thing of all was that the topmost card seemed familiar to me.

I stared at it in disbelief. The card showed a group of girls in long loose robes dancing with garlands of flowers, and as I gazed it seemed not so much that I had seen the card before as that I had *dreamed* it. Impossible. How could I have dreamed of a tarot card when I've never even seen a pack? Mum disapproves of fortune-telling even more than she does astrology. But these could be nothing but the tarot, and I'd just found them in her box.

I picked up the bag again, running my fingers over the embroidered symbols – and there was my answer. A carefully cross-stitched name, flanked by two stars.

NATASHA MUNRO.

Mum's maiden name.

A long shaft of dusty sunlight, which had been clocking its way across the floor, reached my knee and illuminated the tiny stitches.

The cards belonged to Mum. Mum who won't even read her tea leaves and who switches off the TV whenever there's a programme on ghosts or telepathy or mysterious predictions. And yet she had once owned a tarot pack! And not just owned it, but valued it. The bag was so beautifully embroidered and the cards so well worn.

I fanned out the pack, enjoying the procession of magical images – a woman taming a lion, an angel holding a cup. Mum must have spread these cards out, as I was doing now, yet she'd never even hinted that she could read the tarot.

I stared at the cards as though they might hold the answer to this riddle – and then they leaped out of my hands and spilled across the floor. Mum had seized my wrist and was jerking me to my feet.

'What's that you're meddling with?'

I'd been so engrossed that I hadn't heard her come up the stairs, far less cross the room to my side.

'Where did you find those? Will you never learn to leave well alone?'

'I'm sorry, Mum,' I said. I was so taken aback that my voice came out in a childish whine. 'I didn't know there was anything secret in there.'

'I didn't say it was a secret, did I – just none of your business.' Mum had actually gone pale the way redheads do, all her freckles standing out like tiny islands on her white face.

'I've said I'm sorry. I was just trying to help. I thought we could throw some of this stuff out.'

'You've no business to be going through my things.'

'But I didn't know they were *your* things – I mean, half of that stuff belongs to Dad.'

'That still doesn't give you the right to pry.' And Mum began to scoop up the cards.

I bent down to help her, but she actually slapped my hand away, and the card I'd picked up, a grim-faced Queen holding an upright sword, fluttered down between us.

'I can manage, thank you very much. You go and start on the bathroom.'

However, before I could retreat there was a noise outside

which could only be a large removal van squeezing down a narrow road.

'Listen, it's the van,' I said unnecessarily.

'And about time too! What are you waiting for? Go and let the men in.'

So I had to turn away and go downstairs, leaving Mum still scrabbling the cards together with shaking hands.

CHAPTER two

The movers were a gang of cheery musclemen plus a tiny, ancient, gloomy gaffer. The gaffer eyed all our furniture, which looked scuffed and tatty now it had been torn away from its old home, and declared mournfully that 'Yon wardrobe'll never make it up the stair' or 'If the legs willna unscrew we'll have to try the window.' Then, just when Mum was ready to burst into tears, the young lads would coax the furniture round the difficult corner, giving merry cries of 'Easy your end, Jimmie' or such like. Then the sorrowful boss would fix his attention on the next of our possessions and the whole performance would start again.

Anyway, by the time Dad came home – yes, I'd have to learn to call this miserable wee box home – most of the furniture was roughly in place while the sitting room was stacked solid with the tea chests containing his beloved books.

Dad himself was standing happily in the garden, leaning on his bike and tipping the removal men with handfuls of fivers. Even the old boss had livened up – and not just at the prospect of pints of free bevvy. Dad has the knack of making friends instantly. He's one of those people who can walk into a boring party and in a couple of minutes he's got everyone playing charades or singing 'The Wild Rover'.

Anyway, he was now praising the men as though they'd hauled our things over the Alps by elephant – 'Great job you did there, getting that wardrobe round the bend in the stair, hur hur hur' – and the gaffer was saying how nice it was to see real furniture for a change and not yon DIY varnished pine. Then, after a bit of football blether, the young guys nipped briskly into the van, pulled the old boss in after them, and off they drove, presumably making straight for their favourite pub before Dad's money settled down in their pockets and got to feeling at home.

Dad, however, didn't immediately rush inside to inspect his new nest. He leaned his bike up against the wall and revolved slowly, taking deep breaths of the famous fresh air.

'So what do you think?' I said, padding down the path and then looking up at him. Dad is about 23 centimetres taller than I am, and thus a whole 30 centimetres taller than Mum.

'Wonderful,' he said. 'We should've done this years ago.'

'But, Dad, you always said that when you actually lived in the country you couldn't wait to grow up and get into the city.'

'Och, I was just a daft laddie then, didn't know what was good for me.'

'And I thought you liked being near the school and all your old folksy pubs.' Dad, I am sorry to say, is a folk-music buff. 'Now you won't be able to have a bevvy when you go to a ceilidh because of the drive back.'

'If I have one too many, I can crash out on someone's floor.'

He was looking positively happy at the prospect, imagining himself as a dashing student again.

'"Crash out"?' I said, wincing. 'Anyway, I can't see Mum curling up on somebody's carpet.'

'Then she can abstain from the hard stuff and do the driving,' he said, putting on a fake Highland accent. Then he continued, still in the daft voice, 'But are the hills no' bonny, my dark Rosaleen?'

'Dark Rosaleen' is the old Irish song I'm named after. Some band played it at the folk concert at which Mum and Dad met, and they thought it so romantic that I got landed with the name, although I'm usually just called Rosa. Unfortunately, as Mum's name, Natasha, is shortened to Tasha, put together we sound like a country-and-western duo.

Anyway, I had to admit that the hills facing us would be quite pretty if you could ignore the cluster of corrugated-iron farm buildings halfway up the slope. And, of course, our new red home and the two rows of exactly similar neighbours, each with its painfully neat front garden.

'It's OK,' I said, as cheerfully as possible. 'It's just a bit quiet.'

'I know.' Dad dropped back into his ordinary voice and slung his arm round my shoulders. 'It's not fair that you didn't have a choice.'

I leaned against the tweed jacket that he wears as a sort of joke because it's what teachers are supposed to wear, and I sighed. I knew that he was making the best of things and that I ought to do the same. Or I would, if I were the sort of noble, self-sacrificing person who raises money for charity or spends their weekends visiting old people. And if this was my opportunity to find out whether I could be that sort of person, I was able to guess in advance what my answer would be. After all, I'd barely been in the new house five minutes before I'd upset Mum by finding the cards.

Yet she'd been more than upset. Even when Grandad died, Mum had been unhappy in a normal sort of way, not white and raging as she'd been this morning.

I wished I could tell Dad about my discovery, but what if Mum had kept the cards a secret from him as well as from me? That was simply too unnerving to think about.

'But you'll get choices soon enough,' continued Dad, obviously unable to follow my train of silent thought.

'Yeah.' That didn't cheer me up much. I already seemed to be positively *hounded* by choices. Would I try to like my new home? What subjects would I do next year? Which university would I apply to? Would I take a year out? Sometimes all I knew was what I didn't want to do, which was to be like Mum and get married straight away and have kids.

'Are you two going to stand outside for ever?' Mum had appeared in the dinky little porch, hands on trim denim hips. I looked at her carefully for signs of emotion, but she was acting brisk and normal. 'There's the beds to be made up and Nairn's room has to be hoovered and the kitchen stuff unpacked and it'll only be something frozen for supper.'

'Oh bliss, bliss!' cried Dad. 'Oven-fresh, low-fat, crinkle-cut chips! Newly picked, freshly frozen, vitamin-packed, minted baby peas! Oh delicacies dear to my heart! Don't apologize, woman.'

'Come away in, you blether,' said Mum, her bad temper melting, as it always does, in the relentless sunny glow of Dad's personality.

'Shall I carry you over the threshold?' Dad had left me with an affectionate tug of my hair, and was towering lovingly over Mum.

'Don't be ridiculous, it's far too late for that, I've been in and out a dozen times by now.'

'But a symbolic hoist!'

'No, no, watch your back, Davie!'

'Light as a feather!'

And Dad having swept Mum into the house, I tramped in after them. Perhaps I *could* be a super-helpful daughter – but that wasn't going to stop me from having another look at the cards. If they were still there. I'd take the hoover upstairs and then rummage in the box.

But it was as I'd suspected. The blue velvet bag had gone.

I looked around the room. All our old furniture seemed misplaced and unhappy, looming against the pretty pastel wallpaper. Bed, wardrobe, chest of drawers. Mum would have a lot more difficulty concealing the cards here than in our old flat, with its nooks and crannies. But suddenly I didn't have the heart to start searching.

Instead, I wandered over to the window and stared at the supposedly bonny hills. But all I saw was the row of boxy houses opposite – and a solitary figure crossing the field that rose up behind them.

It was the boy from the bridge. I pushed up the sash and leaned out to get a better view. It seemed to me that the further away he went, the more slowly he walked. And as he approached the band of dark woodland that bordered the field, he actually stopped, as though he didn't want to cross the boundary between the open grassland and whatever the trees concealed.

And then he turned round and looked directly towards me, and I jerked back inside. Could he possibly have seen me? Surely not. But if he had, then he'd caught me staring at him twice in one day – as though there was anything the least bit attractive or interesting about him. Of course there wasn't. It was just natural to be curious about new neighbours – because, I thought with a pleasurable sense of shock, that's what he must be if he was still hanging around. A neighbour. So I would see him again. Of course, he probably went to the local school – when he wasn't skiving – and I was staying on at my old high school, but if he was in the habit of going down to the river—

'Rosa! I don't hear the hoover, what's keeping you? Nairn'll be back any minute!' Mum's voice, from the foot of the stairs, brought me back to earth.

'OK, Mum, just getting it out of the box,' I shouted, but before I could actually do so, I heard a whisper of sound from outside. I went back to the window in time to see the stately BMW bearing my little brother, his best friend, Gavin, and Gavin's mum come to the gentlest of halts outside our humble front gate. Nairn then climbed out of the car and waved to Gavin, who, despite going to a posh private school, is actually quite an inoffensive little boy. The reason that he and Nairn are friends is because they both go to Junior Youth Orchestra. Gavin, meanwhile, leaned out of the car and waved back dramatically as though he were abandoning his friend to a lonely life in the wilderness, which, come to think of it, was almost true as Nairn, unlike me, was changing to the local school. However, as, *un*like me, he attracts mates wherever he goes, this wasn't actually such a big deal.

Anyway, Gavin and his mum having driven off, Nairn came running up the path in his favoured designer sports wear, clutching his violin case. Then I could hear him asking if he could go up and see his new room and Mum saying no, it hadn't been hoovered yet. At this, I felt a bit guilty, so I hauled the dustmite-devourer out of its box and plugged it in.

Nairn, however, wasn't complaining, as most kids would've done, but was saying mildly that in that case, he'd go and explore outside. If he were a character in one of Dad's adored Victorian novels, my little brother would be one of those children who die tragically young, words of comfort and cheer upon their pale lips. Personally, I think his noble character has been formed by having to live with a name like Nairn, which is the place Mum's father came from in the north of Scotland. She couldn't just call him

John, which was Grandad's name, as that wasn't swish enough. In fact, it was exactly the same as Grannie calling her little girl Natasha. Her family just like fancy names.

So I brooded about names while I hoovered. What went with long dark hair and a leather jacket? Brendan, Liam, Jude?

So by the time I'd finished, I'd worked myself into a better temper, which was improved even more by Dad producing a bottle of champagne. Mum, who was equally cheered by the sight, put supper on the table just as Nairn came dashing in to say that he'd met a girl *exactly* his age called Karen, who lived at the end of the row and went to his new school. So I'd been right in thinking that his solitary ordeal wouldn't last long. All of forty minutes, in fact.

Mum asked me to pull the curtains before I sat down, but Dad stopped her.

'Look at the lights, Tasha. Let's enjoy our new vista.'

He was right. The autumn twilight had fallen early, and from our vantage point on the hill we could see the lights of Edinburgh shining all the way down to the Forth, then more lights on the far side, and the two glittering bridges linking them together. And as all the nasty things that were lurking in the hollow below us – a derelict factory, an entire cemetery of dead cars – were now hidden from sight, we could almost have been in the real countryside, looking out on a distant city.

I wished I were Nairn's age, so that I could find the whole thing exciting. However, Dad had poured the champagne, so I picked up my glass and raised it as he gave the toast: 'To number one, Burnshead, and all who sail in her!'

As we clinked glasses, my glance drifted back to the dark windowpane. To anyone hiding out there among the trees, we must've been clearly visible. If this were a movie, the laughing, innocent family would be set up for disaster as surely as the good black cop always gets killed.

'Can't I draw the curtains now?' I said. 'Anyone out there could see in.'

'And who's going to be out there?' laughed Dad. 'Have you got an admirer already? You're a dark horse, dark Rosaleen!'

I stiffened at Dad's teasing. The boy on the bridge hadn't thought I was worth looking at, far less admiring.

'If this were *Little House on the Prairie*,' said Nairn, naming a favourite bedtime book, 'there would be Red Indians out there and we could shoot them from the window.' He made Kalashnikov noises. Nairn may be unusually sweet-natured, but in some ways he's no different from any other kid.

'That's Native Americans,' said Dad, in his most teacherly voice, 'and it wouldn't have been that sort of gun. You'd have had to pick them off one by one as they crept through the trees. And there would've been dozens of them, coming nearer and nearer, taunting you into wasting ammunition, knowing that eventually you'd run out of food and water—'

'What a thing to be talking about at our first meal!' cried Mum, placing the dishes of now toastie frozen food on the table. 'It'll bring bad luck.'

Mum is one of these people who always put spiders tenderly outside because she believes it's unlucky to kill them, and she'd rather step out into a busy road than walk under a ladder. And then it struck me: if Mum was so superstitious, why did she not believe in fortune-telling and astrology? Surely it ought to be the other way round – she ought to be the sort of person who read teacups and rushed to look up her horoscope every month. But she wasn't.

I stared at the happy scene in front of me, wondering if it really was so happy. Was Mum pretending to be light-hearted, or was she brooding over my discovery, just as I was?

'I thought you wanted to pull the curtains?' Mum's voice broke into my reverie. 'Now I've got the idea of Indians out there it looks downright creepy.'

At that Dad and I began to laugh and Nairn gave wild war whoops while I pulled the curtains on the Native American-infested undergrowth.

'Nah, nah,' said Dad. 'I can tell you what would be a deal scarier, son – silence, dead silence, with now and again the cry of an owl. But is it really an owl? And isn't it awful near?'

'Or drum beats, Dad, down by the river.' Nairn began to beat a tattoo on the table while Dad did a really naff owl impression.

'Stop your nonsense, both of you!' But Mum was laughing as well, and our first meal at Burnshead had got off to an apparently cheery start.

CHAPTER three

'Hey, Rosie, what do you think, Franklin's asked me out on a date! Isn't that totally wonderful?'

Debs, who is my best friend and the only person in the world to call me Rosie, came bouncing down the school steps. As she bounced, her curly brown hair bobbed along with her, and her big brown eyes gleamed. All this enthusiasm is usually rather endearing, but today I was irritated. I'd moved house the day before, something Debs knew I'd been dreading, and here she was, yattering about Franklin, that big useless lump, instead of being properly interested in my exile.

'He walked up the road with me to the deli yesterday lunchtime, and he told me all about this place his parents have in Virginia. Virginia! Isn't that romantic?'

Franklin is an American guy who is at our school while his father teaches some course at the nearby university. We have several foreign kids in our class for this reason, and while they generally make life more interesting and exotic, Franklin, in my opinion, is a gigantic exception.

'So what else did you talk about?' I said sarcastically, backing away from a game of playground football. 'The economy, the Euro, the state of democracy in the land of the free?' Franklin is as thick as he is tall, blond and handsome.

Debs, however, ignored my comments and went on bouncing, hugging her jacket across her Wonderbra-enhanced chest. She likes to flaunt everything she's got, and today was wearing, beneath her wee denim jacket, a tight V-necked sweater and slinky trousers, in contrast to my usual big furry top and jeans.

'I just couldn't believe it when he asked me out! And you should've seen Marisa and Leanne – they kept trying to butt into our conversation and he just totally ignored them.'

'Like you're doing to me now,' I said.

'Sorry, what?' Debs stopped in mid flow, looking puzzled, like a puppy who doesn't understand why it's being scolded.

'Yes, thank you, Debs, the move went very well,' I said. 'Of course, it does take me for ever to get in on the bus, but I'll get used to it.'

'Oh, Rosie, I'm sorry!' wailed Debs, her eyes opening even wider in distress. 'I forgot all about your flitting. Was everything all right? Is it really out in the country?'

'You can see for yourself on Saturday,' I said. 'You're going to come out then, right?'

'Well, I don't know if I can make it *this* Saturday.' Debs lowered her bag from her shoulder and swung it casually from one hand to the other.

I was stunned. 'But what do you mean, you can't come?

You said you were going to come the first Saturday after I'd moved!'

Debs looked at me with huge, pleading eyes. 'I know, but the thing is, I might be going to see Franklin play.' Franklin is on the basketball team. 'They've got a match on down in Leith.'

Although she was looking at me so innocently, Debs wriggled a bit as she said this.

'So what about Sunday then?'

'Sunday I said I'd go out with Mum. You know I really want to come, but I've promised her.'

I wanted to say that she had also promised me for Saturday, but as everyone knows the rule is that boyfriends come first, I kept quiet.

'So next weekend then?' Debs gave me her old happy-go-lucky smile, knowing that I'd forgive her.

I wasn't so sure. I suddenly felt completely fed up with having my good nature always taken for granted. It was bad enough feeling that I had to be cheerful and understanding at home without having to be these things with Debs as well.

'I suppose so,' I said. 'If I haven't anything else on.'

'But what might you have on? I thought you said it was the absolute ends of the earth out there. I thought you said there was totally nothing to do.'

I remembered the boy on the bridge and his reluctant disappearance into the wood. I remembered his brief glance at me, and I smiled mysteriously. 'You never know. There may be possibilities.'

'Possibilities of what?'

'Too early to say.' And I climbed the steps into the crowded hall, leaving Debs to trot along behind me.

It was only when we were in class that I remembered that I'd meant to tell her about Mum's tarot. Well, I decided, Debs didn't *deserve* to be told. Just let her stew along with her wonderful Franklin.

When school was over, I went to get a bus downtown instead of going straight home. Clary, who is my reading-and-filmgoing friend, saw me at the bus stop and paused, her arms full of books and ringbinders. She always seems to be carrying more of these than other people, which is perhaps due to the fact that both her parents are academics and expect her to carry on the family tradition.

'What are you doing at this stop? I thought your new place was in the opposite direction.'

At least *someone* had noticed that I'd moved house. 'Just nipping downtown to get a book.'

Her eyes lit up at the word 'book'. 'Which book?'

I realized I'd made a mistake here. I hadn't confided my new-found interest in the tarot to Debs, who is my oldest friend – we used to play in the back green together – yet here I was about to let it slip to Clary. There was no point in lying, because, like Dad, books are her speciality, and if I said I'd bought a particular novel, for instance, she'd be bound to ask me later how I was enjoying it.

'I'm just going to look for something on the tarot.'

'The *tarot*?' Clary looked down her long and distinguished nose.

'Why not?' I said, aware that I was beginning to blush. Clary is quite difficult to be friends with because she won't take into account other people's low and vulgar tastes. The opposite of Debs, in fact, whose own vulgar taste had led her to settle on Franklin.

'Why not?' I repeated more defensively. 'I just want to find out more about its history.'

'But why?' echoed Clary, freeing one hand from her books to push back her toffee-coloured plait. 'It's just superstition to think that a pack of cards can foretell your future. In fact, it's worse, because you're giving up your free will and capacity for rational thought by depending upon an *irrational* practice.'

Put like that there didn't seem much point in saying that I'd intuitively recognized the very first card I'd picked up, or that the cards had seemed to want me to find them, so I muttered, 'I only got interested because I came across a pack recently. I just wanted to find out a bit more about them.'

'Well, watch your step,' said Clary darkly, looking at me as though I were a severe disappointment to her. This, she was obviously thinking, wasn't the girl who sneaked out of PE with her to go to our local art cinema. 'If you're not careful, you'll get sucked right in. First thing the tarot, next thing astrology – before you know it you won't be able to make a move without consulting some oracle.'

'I only meant I was interested in their history,' I said feebly, but Clary looked disbelieving.

'It's the first step on a *downward path*. Don't say I didn't warn you!' And sounding exactly like an oracle herself, she turned round and disappeared among a crowd of juniors, her bag of books bumping over her shoulder and her plait hanging absolutely straight down the centre of her back.

I sighed. First Mum, now Clary. But that tarot pack had once meant something to Mum, something important, and even if I couldn't find out what, I could dig around the edges of the mystery. I thought again of the beautiful card which I'd seemed to recognize. Surely the garlanded maidens couldn't do me any harm?

Yet, remembering Mum's white face, I gave a little shiver as I climbed onto the bus. This was just research, as I'd told Clary, historical research.

The shop had several books on the tarot, so I chose the simplest and then hurried to catch the bus home. Once I'd found a seat beside a woman walled in by M & S Food Hall bags, I pulled out my purchase and began to flick eagerly through the pages. Yes, there were all the images which had fallen through my fingers as Mum whipped the cards away from me. The Priestess, the Empress, then a hooded skeleton with a scythe – I turned back to the beginning and began to read properly.

The tarot, I discovered, has four suits – Wands, Swords, Cups and Pentangles – but the really interesting cards are the extra twenty-two, the Major Arcana. They show symbolic figures like Death and Strength and Judgement and they were banished by the Church, which thought they were the work of the Devil – rather like Clary! But the forbidden cards never quite disappeared. The gypsies kept the art of divination alive, and the ancient magic lived on in their caravans as they crossed Europe from fair to fair, telling fortunes as they travelled.

It all sounded terribly romantic. Mum had once followed in the gypsy tradition and perhaps I was meant to do the same, despite Clary's black warnings. Then, as the bus came to a halt, I was jolted back to the present. Where was I? I peered through the fogged-up window, panicking in case I'd been carried beyond my stop, and, to my relief, recognized the local supermarket. One more stop to go. As I sank back, I saw someone who had just got off the bus drift past me and go into the store.

It was the boy from the bridge. Although it was almost dark, and although he was now wearing old-fashioned flannels and a private-school blazer, there was no mistaking him. If nothing else, I would've known him by his contemptuous slouch as he turned and shouldered his way through the swing door, exactly as he'd turned to let me pass him on the bridge.

As the bus moved on again, I found myself rubbing the windowpane and staring back into the dusk, almost as though I still expected to see that thin dark face on the other side of the glass. So what shopping was he doing on the way home from school? And what a school! I'd recognized the blazer at once. Very posh, very expensive; his parents must be loaded. What would they think if they knew that he was wasting their money by lounging about by the river, watching girls and smoking, when he ought to be preparing for a career as a lawyer or a doctor?

The bus was slowing again, so I shoved the tarot book into my bag and jumped off. As I strode up the hill, passing prim bungalows, I wondered what sort of house my intriguing neighbour lived in, and if he always took that particular bus, and what, if we ever met, we'd say to one another. Because surely we were bound to meet, both living in this lonely outpost of civilization? Although, of course, after the rude way he'd treated me on the bridge, I might choose not to speak to him at all – then I realized that I'd left the houses behind and was climbing the wooded gorge at the top of which lay our little estate. This was the first time I'd walked up the road, so I hadn't realized how menacing it would be as night fell.

I walked faster and faster, my trainers making a nervous, scuttling sound against the horribly unidentifiable country noises. Why ever had I stayed late in town to buy that wretched book? If I'd caught the earlier bus, it would still have been light. Clary was correct. My first step on the path of the tarot was a dark and scary one.

CHAPTER four

'Mum, it's awful dark coming up the hill there,' I said, once I was safely in the kitchen, a cup of coffee in one hand and a piece of Grannie's famous shortbread in the other. I was standing at the window, looking back down the way I'd just come, although the actual road was hidden by the curve of the hill and the gloomy tangled wood.

Grannie, who was drinking tea at the table after a happy day helping Mum hang curtains and unpack boxes, said, 'Aye, Tasha, you dinna want the lassie to walk up yon hill in the dark.'

Mum, busy at the sink, sighed. 'Of course not, but it's not really dark, there's lights all the way.'

'It is so too,' I said, momentarily forgetting to be cheerful. 'It's really creepy in among the trees.'

'Oh, Rosa, I'm sorry,' said Mum, taking her sudsy hands out of the water and clasping them together. 'I could come down and meet you in the car if you gave me a call. That's what your mobile's for.' Then her pretty face puckered up still further. 'But it would mean taking

Nairn with me. I can't leave him in the house by himself.'

'Yes you can,' said Nairn, appearing round the door, his eyes dark-rimmed from battling with computer dragons. 'I'm not a baby. What's going to happen to me?'

I could literally see the black thoughts chasing each other behind Mum's worried face. The house might burst into flames. Masked intruders might break in and abduct her wee darling. The woods might just, after all, be crawling with murderous redskins.

'Come on, Mum, be logical,' said Nairn. Dad is always appealing to logic. 'What could possibly happen to me, sitting quietly in my own home?'

Mum opened and shut her mouth a couple of times and then brought out triumphantly, 'But it's illegal, leaving a child of your age alone, that's what. So logic doesn't come into it.'

I could see Nairn revving himself up for one of his smarty-pants answers, so I said quickly, 'Don't worry, Mum. It only seemed dark tonight because I missed the first bus.' I certainly wasn't going to tell her why I'd missed it. 'I'll be quicker getting to the stop tomorrow.'

'If you really think so . . .' said Mum doubtfully, but she still looked worried. 'If we had a second car, Dad could drive to work and pick you up on the way home.' Dad doesn't teach at my school, thank goodness, but at one nearby. He'd been declaring, however, that not only could we not afford another car, but we certainly didn't need one, as he was going to cycle into work every day along the river path. Mum needs the car to get round her customers, as she does home hairdressing. 'When he comes in, you tell him how dark it is.'

'No, it's OK, Mum, it's not really so bad,' I said, not wanting to get manipulated into a family argument. Mum sometimes seems to think that because Dad went to university and she didn't, she doesn't have any right to her own opinion.

'But we can't have you walking up yon hill in the dark,' repeated Grannie, with dramatic relish.

'These woods might be full of muggers,' said Nairn, with equal enjoyment.

'I said, it won't be so dark if I catch the early bus,' I repeated sharply.

'But the nights are drawing in,' said Grannie. You'd almost think she wanted me to be in danger because of the excitement of it. I could imagine her eagerly describing my perilous journey to all her old lady friends at the community centre.

'But this is the *country*,' said Mum, as though criminals stopped politely at the city boundary. She had dried her hands and was now setting the table. 'It's going to be a much healthier life out here for Rosa and Nairn.'

Oh yes? I wanted to say sarcastically. Healthy? Squashed on a smelly bus every day, breathing up other people's disgusting winter germs? But I didn't, as staying at my old school had been my own choice. I couldn't bear the thought of starting over again. I'm not like Nairn and Dad, popular wherever they go. I mean, Nairn isn't even good at games, because of his wheezing, and he's *still* popular.

'Och, I know you had to move,' said Grannie. 'It's just a pity it had to be so far away.'

Mum made hushing noises behind Nairn's back. He's not supposed to know that anyone's upset at leaving the heart of historic Edinburgh for his sake.

'I think it's just lovely out here,' she said. 'I can hardly wait for summer, to see what's going to come up in the garden.'

Nairn, however, had picked up on the ripple of discomfort. 'Do you really like it here?' he said, suddenly looking thinner and paler than usual.

'Of course I do,' said Mum, ruffling his ultra-fashionable haircut. He and Grannie are the only members of the family to allow Mum to practise her professional skills upon them. Dad and I prefer a natural look – although he gets a forcible trim when his curls start getting into his ears.

I tried to say that I also thought it was great, but the words just wouldn't come out of my mouth. So instead I said, 'How was the new school? How's the girlfriend?'

'Karen. She's nice. She's got red hair, like Mum's, and what d'you think, a boy called Ed asked me to be in his gang and his dad's a mountaineer and when I go round to his house, Ed's going to show me his dad's climbing stuff.'

As Nairn launched into a description of his new friends, I looked around the table. There was Mum in her jeans and a fifties crossover pinny she'd got in Flip, her gorgeous hair pinned up into a nest of curls; Grannie in a pastel cardigan and slacks, her grey thatch neatly permed; and then me, hiding inside my dark jersey, with my mop of hair clipped into a bunch. Then I wondered what Mum would look like if she'd gone on being a tarot reader? Would she be draped in black velvet, with loads of Goth jewellery?

That was so seriously unlikely that I almost smiled. Mum is a big charity shop dresser but her outfits are stylish, in her own weird way, rather than hippy.

However, my thoughts were interrupted by Dad marching in, brandishing his cycling helmet with a tremendous air of healthy self-satisfaction.

'I made record time along the river – it's going to be wonderful in the spring.'

'But what about the winter, Davie? You'll never keep it up all through the winter.'

'Just watch me, Tasha!'

'But is it not awful dark down by the river?' That was Grannie, obviously.

'No, no, I never mind the dark, I just ride on like Tam o' Shanter.'

Tam o' Shanter is the hero of one of Dad's favourite Scottish poems.

'But you mind what happened to him?' said Grannie. 'Chased by witches!'

This was such an unlikely fate for Dad that we all burst out laughing.

First Native Americans, now witches; it seemed that my family were determined to turn the woods into a really exciting place. Whereas the only person whom I *knew* to be lurking there was the boy in the black leather jacket, and actually, he seemed quite exciting enough.

While we were still chuckling, and Dad was splashing water over his glowing face and hands, Mum began to put the supper on the table.

'Yuck, courgettes!' said Nairn, screwing up his face. 'Why do we have to have courgettes, Mum? They're so slimy.'

'I bet Gavin has them all the time,' I said.

'That continental touch, very nice,' said Grannie. Now that she's a senior citizen, Grannie has become the family traveller. While we go to cold, damp places with folk festivals, like Brittany or Ireland, lucky old Grannie gets to sit in the sun. 'I do enjoy a nice bit of courgette. Now, Rosa, why don't you pull the curtains, and we can eat our dinner without feeling that anyone could be looking in.'

Because it was Grannie speaking, Dad didn't object as he had the previous evening, and I went over to the window. While my back was turned, Mum took the opportunity to say to Dad, 'Rosa was fair frightened coming up the hill there in the dark. Now, if we had a second car—'

'I was not frightened!' I declared, whisking round and pulling the curtains in one furious movement. Why had I ever raised the subject in the first place?

'The thing to do is for Rosa to get a bike,' said Dad. 'Then we can ride home together. Problem solved.'

I actually found my eyes filling with tears of exasperation. Dad, like all other cyclists, invariably thinks that having a bike will solve all life's problems.

'I don't *want* a bike, thank you,' I said, as politely as possible. 'I'm just not a bike person.'

'Now that's not very grateful to your father,' said Grannie. 'When I was your age, I'd've loved a bike.'

'Then why doesn't Dad give *you* the bike?' I snapped.

There was a nasty moment of embarrassed silence. Then Nairn said, 'Don't cry, Rosa,' and came and threw his arms around my waist, the sort of un-little-brotherly action which makes me definitely think he is lined up for an early grave.

'I'm not crying,' I said, brushing my hot pink cheeks. 'Sorry, Grannie.'

'We'll say no more about it,' said Grannie, but with a sniffish, offended air which let us all know that even if she didn't mention it again now, the incident might well reappear in the future.

'Let's all have our supper while it's hot,' said Mum firmly. She likes everything to be *nice* – no one expressing unpleasant emotions, no matter what they might be feeling underneath.

And, in fact, as I went to sit down, Nairn still giving me loving little pats, I wasn't sure *what* I was feeling. It wasn't about the bike or the dark, it was more about not seeing Edinburgh Castle from my bedroom window any more, and Debs forgetting I'd moved, and Clary being so disapproving about the cards, and the cards themselves, and Mum's furious hands, slapping at mine.

I looked across the table at Nairn, who was arranging his courgettes in a neat frill around the edge of his plate, and my depression deepened. Not only was he brighter and more popular than me, but he could play all the Scottish fiddle music that Mum and Dad love so much.

I couldn't play anything and I'm only averagely clever, and I'd broken my vow of being cheerful on the second day in the new house!

I was obviously a complete wash-out as a daughter and the sooner either the Native Americans or the Scottish witches got me, the better.

CHAPTER five

It was a quiet, polite sort of meal in contrast to all the fun we'd had the night before. Everyone was trying hard to forget my tearful outburst, but it had left an uncomfortable feeling in the air. The moment supper was over, Dad rushed off into the dining room, which he was colonizing as his study, Nairn went with him to do his homework on the computer, and Mum prepared to give Grannie a lift home. It felt like no one wanted to be in my presence a moment longer than necessary in case I Made a Scene, which is not a McBride thing to do.

Anyway, when Grannie saw Mum putting on her coat, she whisked into her humble-little-old-lady routine. 'Och, Tasha, don't you bother to give me a lift. I can get the bus just fine.'

'Don't be daft, Mum! And walk down thon dark hill!'

I thought that if I heard one more word about the hill and how dark it was, I would scream, so I said quickly that I'd do the dishes while Mum was away.

'But haven't you got homework?'

'They'll only take a minute.'

'Don't bother with the pans, then, just leave them to soak.' And before Grannie could raise any more objections about the lift she'd always intended taking, Mum had hustled her off, and I was left alone in the kitchen.

I took another piece of Grannie's shortie and munched it gloomily. On one side of me I could hear the car starting up in the garage, and on the other a favourite CD of Dad's, an old hippy folk singer named Fergie Mac. I hadn't *meant* to be upset. I hadn't meant to *show* I was upset. I was trying to be brave and cheery and all that stuff but I really hated my new home and everything about it, and most of all I hated being brought here against my will.

And no one seemed to care! Well, Nairn had cared, but Mum and Dad and Grannie had just rushed to smooth over my hurt feelings as though they didn't exist. Mum and Grannie, especially, like things to be *nice* – but *life* isn't nice! You never know when something's going to jump up and hit you. Like moving house. Or finding the tarot cards. The thought of the cards almost made me rush upstairs – Mum out, Dad and Nairn busy, the perfect moment to renew my search – but the dirty dishes brought me up short. I couldn't make things worse by letting Mum come back to a midden. So I washed and dried everything, including the pans, and only then did I slip upstairs and open the door to Mum and Dad's bedroom.

The curtains hadn't been drawn but, as I raised my hand, I saw a light glimmering through the trees, just beyond where the boy had disappeared yesterday. Not a solid bright square like the windows of the houses opposite, but a gleam so faint that it made me picture an old mansion, roof falling in, walls held up by ivy, and someone inside drifting from window to window, holding a candle up to each cracked and dusty pane.

The image was so real that it was a shock to wake up and find myself with one hand locked to a fold of curtain, staring into the night. I was going completely mental. If there was a light beyond the trees, it only meant another estate of new houses. I'd go and explore on Saturday. After all, if my so-called best friend was standing me up for a basketball game, I'd have nothing better to do. And if I happened to run into that boy, it wouldn't mean that I'd been hoping to meet him.

I pulled the curtains shut and turned towards the room. Where would Mum have hidden the cards? Although I felt sneaky and uneasy, poking about behind her back, I told myself that if only she'd *explained*, then I wouldn't have to do this. It was her own fault that I was rummaging around her bedroom.

Nothing in her underwear drawer, too obvious. Nor beneath the mattress, for the same reason.

Searching at random wasn't doing me any good. I stopped in the centre of the room and imagined Mum, blue velvet bag in hand, standing where I was now and looking for a good hiding place.

Then I concentrated upon the bag itself, trying to see it as I'd seen the ghostly house. But this was something real. Thick dark velvet, the top drawn tight with a blue cord, a cord which was long enough to loop over something – of course! I couldn't tell how I knew, but I was certain of it.

I crossed the room to the wardrobe, a huge, curly thing which had once belonged to Grannie and Grandad. I saw my reflection in the mirror on the door as I approached, and I could almost have been the figure in my make-believe mansion, gliding over the floor, hand upraised, eyes staring. I swung back the door and looked along the row of clothes inside. Dad isn't really into fashion, so his end contained only his good suit and some tatty old cords and jeans. Mum, on the other hand, not only loves clothes but never gets rid of them, so most of the interior was crammed with her huge collection of outfits, from brand new to retro. I checked them off along the rail until I reached the wafty chiffon number with satin trim which Mum had worn on her first real date with Dad. She'd often told me the story of how he'd invited her to a friend's wedding, and how the reception had been held in a beautiful garden where they'd drunk champagne and wandered through glades of roses. And although Mum, at the time, was only a hairdresser's apprentice, she hadn't felt a bit out of place because her dress, made by Grannie from a Vogue pattern, was the prettiest there.

And this symbolic gown was the one she had chosen as the hiding place for her tarot cards. There was the cord, looped round the hanger, and there, swinging discreetly under the bodice, the velvet bag. It seemed the most natural thing in the world to unhook the cord, reach my hand up through the cool layers of chiffon, and let the small, definite weight drop into my hand. And at the exact moment that my fingers closed around it, I heard a door open downstairs and Mum's voice:

'Rosa, I said to leave the pans!'

I shoved the dress back into the wardrobe, slammed the door once, and then twice as the old clasp refused to catch, leaped over the bedroom floor and ran on tiptoe to my own room. Without time to be ingenious, I pushed the bag under my pillow, and then sauntered to the top of the stairs.

'It's OK, Mum, they weren't very dirty,' I called.

Mum stuck her head round the kitchen door. 'Thank you all the same. Will I bring you up another coffee?'

'No, thanks, I'm fine. I'll just get on with my homework.'

The last thing I wanted was Mum appearing with a steaming cup in her well-meaning hand, so I retreated to my room and shut the door loudly behind me. Then I sat down on my bed and took the bag out from under the pillow. Just as it had done when I first found it, the velvet felt almost alive under my fingers, and each little embroidered symbol stood up crisply against the soft fabric.

Before I actually opened the bag, I took a deep breath and looked around my new room. Like every other inch of this house, it had been decorated by the previous owners with a pastel flowered paper and off-white paint, and I could hardly wait to cover it in a nice deep purple or dark crimson. And perhaps I'd stencil some stars on the ceiling, or signs of the zodiac, or a magic pentangle.

Then I looked down at my hands. Without realizing it,

I had slipped the cards free of their silk wrapping, and they were already fanned out between my fingers, just as though they wanted to be there. And the card on top was a young boy holding a pentangle. Just a coincidence, I told myself. I must have looked down at the card unconsciously, and that had given me the image of a five-pointed star. I couldn't have foreseen two of the cards. I began to flip through them – would I mysteriously recognize any more of the pictures?

Not all the cards were pleasant. One in particular held me with a horrible fascination: a man pierced through by ten swords. He lay under the tilted crosspieces, like a single body granted more than the one necessary grave. Looking at it, I could understand why Mum might be afraid of the tarot. Imagine peering into the future and drawing this card! You might as well jump off the Forth Bridge and be done with it.

Perhaps something like that had happened to Mum. She had drawn an unlucky card and then— Without giving myself time to think I turned the cards over and closed my eyes. 'Please tell me what happened to make Mum give you up,' I whispered. Then I picked a card and opened my eyes – and there, on my patchwork bedspread, lay a black-cloaked skeleton, merrily scything down the tiny, pleading figures who stood in its way.

I didn't need my new book to see what it meant. The Death card! Had Mum once drawn it for herself? But she, obviously, was still alive, and Grandad hadn't died until a couple of years ago. My choosing this card was just another coincidence. I'd been thinking scary thoughts and somehow my subconscious had picked up on them – but even while I was working things out sensibly, my hands, shaking as Mum's had done, were picking up the cards and bundling them away.

Clary had been absolutely right and I hadn't listened to her! I'd put the cards back right now, this very minute, and no matter how tempted I was, I'd never look at them again.

I jumped up and made for the door – just as I heard Dad and Nairn climbing the stairs, Nairn asking Dad if he'd read him a bedtime story, and Dad saying Nairn was too old for all that, but meaning to all the same. Dad loves reading aloud, which meant that he'd be upstairs for at least twenty minutes, and at any one of these minutes he might jink back into his own room to put on his slippers or something.

I clutched the bag, feeling myself turn into one big puddle of indecision. Make a dash for Mum and Dad's room? Hide it somewhere here? Finally I just rushed over to my bookcase and dropped it behind a pile of project folders. There was no point in finding an elaborate hiding place because I would be returning the cards to their home with Mum's old party dress at the first possible moment.

CHAPTER SIX

The next couple of days I kept my promise to myself and didn't look at the cards. But on the other hand, I hadn't returned them to Mum's wardrobe. It just seemed that whenever I was about to do it, either Nairn and some of his new wee pals came racing upstairs, or Mum embarked on a lengthy unpacking and tidying session. In fact, it was almost as though the cards were determined to stay with me. On Friday night I was actually creeping across the hall, the velvet bag clutched behind my back, when Dad came upstairs, tape measure in hand, cheerily announcing that the book overspill was going to wash right into their bedroom and he was going to measure up for new shelves.

'Won't Mum have something to say about that?' I said, edging backwards towards my room. I suspected that Mum's design plan didn't include several hundred dusty old classics. She doesn't exactly dislike books, but thinks they should be kept in their place, and that place is in Dad's study.

'Nonsense, nonsense, culture before comfort,' said Dad,

fortunately so taken up with his new project that he didn't notice my odd behaviour. 'I'll just work out how much shelving I need and then I can pick it up tomorrow.'

Of course, I thought, as I sidled back to safety and placed the cards in their temporary hiding place, tomorrow was Saturday. And the first thing I was going to do was stroll up the hill and see what lay beyond the wood. I drew the curtains back and looked out, as I had every night since my arrival. Yes, there was the faint light, barely visible through the trees. By this time tomorrow, I would know what was there!

However, I'd no sooner got downstairs on Saturday morning and had my tea bag dunked and toast buttered – unlike Mum, I don't believe in dieting – when Mum herself came bustling in wearing a scarf over her hair and her dreaded painting overall.

'Now, Rosa, with Dad and Nairn out of the way, we can get down to business.'

While even in work clothes she may look dainty and flowerlike, when it comes to interior dec Mum is an absolute demon.

'Where have they gone?' I asked feebly. The rats! Obviously they'd taken one look at the pinny and fled.

'Dad's taken Nairn to Gavin's for the day and then he's going for some shelving, so that'll give us a chance to get ahead.'

It wasn't worthwhile asking her get ahead with what. Our old flat had been painted and decorated and stencilled to within an inch of its life, and so Mum could hardly wait to get started on transforming our pastel paradise into something a little more adventurous.

'I saw this great idea on TV for mixing sand with your emulsion, to give that grainy, Mediterranean look,' she was saying, eyes gleaming as she bounded around the kitchen in paint-spattered plimsolls. 'You can get started on the living-room ceiling, Rosa, you're taller.' I always do the ceiling. 'And I'll mix up this Moroccan Rust for the walls.'

Mum is so brilliant at picking colours and putting them together that I've always wondered why she didn't go to art college. Dad once suggested she should do a proper course in interior design, but she was so snippy about it that I've never dared mention the subject. It does seem a huge shame, though, that she should be wasting her talent.

Anyway, I knew better than to utter the words 'art college'; nor did I mention Dad's new shelves and where he was going to put them, in case he hadn't told her yet, so in a couple of shakes of a paintbrush we were working away together to the beat of an old U2 album. Mum would've preferred the droning Fergie Mac, but when I said that his Celtic gloom would slow down my brushstrokes, she compromised on another of her old idols.

Once I'd actually started painting, I remembered all the good times I'd had helping Mum in the past, and I stopped being sorry at having to postpone my expedition. I even stopped brooding over the tarot mystery, and by the time Dad came back with a load of food from our favourite deli and his new shelves, which he left tactfully outside, all the droopy wee flowers had disappeared and Mum's hot hareem look was taking their place.

'Great,' said Dad from the door, looking, as he usually does at first sight of Mum's colour schemes, a bit bewildered.

'It'll be brilliant when we've finished,' Mum said, with total confidence.

'I believe you.'

'Now, Rosa, we can stop for lunch and let the smell clear a bit. Davie, where are you going to put your bookshelves? You know there'll be no room in here once the furniture's back?'

'Well, Tasha, I think they might just have to go upstairs.'

'Upstairs?' cried Mum, as though he were talking about a pack of big, muddy-pawed hounds rather than a few rows of books. 'And just whereabouts upstairs did you have in mind?'

I crept into the kitchen, very quietly made myself an enormous ham and sundried-tomato sandwich and went to sit on the rustic bench at the bottom of the garden. As I ate, bits of Mum and Dad's conversation drifted out of various windows as they moved around the house, examining alternative book sites.

'What's to stop you putting some of them in the garage?'

'You can't put books in a *garage*, woman!'

'But they'll spoil the look of the bedroom. I was going to do it in dark Rustic Rose with a four-poster effect, and books will ruin that.'

I finished my sandwich and stretched my aching arms

and shoulders. There'd be no harm in having a little walk, and by the time I came back Dad would've talked Mum round to his point of view, the usual end to all their arguments. So I took off the old shirt I was wearing over my jumper and jeans and let myself out onto the road. It was a beautiful bright day, and there was a lot of what passed for action in my new neighbourhood. A wee girl in a bright red parka was riding a trike up and down her path, while a couple of young husband types were washing their cars. It was a far cry from the gangs of boys who'd lounged about the pavements at home, or the little Asian girls, in their gorgeous silks, who'd played hopscotch under our windows, so it was with a sigh of nostalgia that I climbed the low stone wall and set off up the hill, heading for the place where the boy had disappeared.

I supposed that in summer it might be more romantic, but at the moment it was just a strip of boring old brown trees, and quite a narrow strip at that, because I'd barely gone a few paces when I saw, dead in front of me, exactly what I had come to find.

I'd found it, but I couldn't believe it. What I'd expected to see was either a single farmhouse, or another spread of new houses. Instead, what I was looking at was the crumbling old turreted mansion I'd imagined when I first saw the faint light. Perhaps not actually falling down, but with ivy overgrowing the upper windows, and a tangle of shrubs darkening those on the ground floor. I almost rubbed my eyes. Had I imagined the house into existence? Of course not. It had obviously been there for centuries, gradually subsiding from a family home into a refuge for mice and woodworm and bats. I had simply recognized it, as I'd recognized some of the tarot cards.

I shivered, digging my hands into the pockets of my jeans. I'd go straight back to my cosy new home without wasting a second glance on this ruin. Certainly it might be possible for a light from the turret windows to be visible from our house, but it was certain that no one – or no one *human* – had lived there for years.

Then, exactly as I was reassuring myself, I saw something move at one of the upper windows. Just a glimpse, a pale face swiftly withdrawn, but I was off through the trees and halfway down the hill before I'd taken a couple of breaths. I stumbled over the grass, my mind veering between two terrible possibilities: either that boy had caught me spying on him again; or I'd seen a ghost. I hardly knew which was worse. Did I prefer looking silly to being haunted?

But my question was already answered. Someone with an unmistakable slouch and untidy black hair was coming up the hill towards me. I slowed down at once to a leisurely walk, hands in pockets, back straight. I knew, though, that I wasn't going to fool anyone. My face felt hot and red, and I wasn't even beginning to get my breath back. My embarrassment would be obvious to a toddler, let alone to the boy who was now strolling towards me, already looking amused. And there was absolutely no chance of escape! Nothing but empty fields to either side of us, and it was too late to turn away without looking even more stupid than I did already. Passing him would only last a second, I told myself, and, after all, I had a perfect right to be rambling about the countryside on such a nice afternoon. I could be looking for wild flowers or rare birds or something.

While I was thinking all of this, we were getting nearer and nearer to one another. The boy was wearing jeans and the same old beaten-up leather jacket over a T-shirt. His face, which I was now seeing properly for the first time, was lean, dark and clever, and his black hair fell forwards into his eyes.

Then, as he approached, I realized something. He was feeling as awkward as I did. I don't know exactly how I could tell, because he was looking at me with a horrible half-smile, exactly as he'd done on the bridge, but it was something about the way in which his hands, like mine, were dug into his pockets, and his eyes kept glancing off to the side. He had a rucksack over one shoulder, and as we finally drew level he hitched it up uncomfortably, further denting his cool.

Aha! I thought. No so confident after all, are we? I inclined my head in what I hoped was a stately manner and sailed on down the hill. Then I managed to climb the wall without falling over, and finished my journey without once looking back.

When I reached our garden, I found that Dad, true to form, was making new friends. He was leaning over the gate and chatting to one of the car-washing men, who was carrying the little girl in red.

'Rosa!' he cried, greeting me as though I'd been gone for weeks. 'Come and meet our new neighbours. Bob, this is my lovely daughter, Rosaleen; Rosa, this is Bob Parker and Molly. They're all the way from Hampshire, so we'll have to show them a real Scottish ceilidh, won't we?'

And then Dad went into his usual embarrassing routine of hugging me and telling Mr Parker what a clever lassie I was, and how I had a nice wee voice if I'd only use it, and how his wife sang like a lintie, and how, while he played the fiddle a bit, his son played like the devil himself.

While Dad was carrying on like this I wished that, no matter how much I loved him, nor how many good qualities he might have, he could just be exterminated in some swift and gruesome fashion. How could he possibly humiliate me like this? Had he no idea how stupid and naff and *jolly* he sounded? And there was no more escape than there had been when I was facing the boy on the hillside. There, at least, I'd been alone, but here I was clasped to Dad's side, his arm tossed chummily round my shoulders.

Mr Parker, however, seemed to be as impressed by Dad as adults usually are. God knows what his pupils think about him (I would definitely rather not know) but other people always seem to perk up in his presence like wilting flowers after a dose of plant food. I finally managed to wriggle away, but I'd barely made it into the kitchen when Mum set upon me, thrusting my paintbrush back into my hand.

'And where did you wander off to, when you know there's work to be done? We've got to get this coat finished before Nairn gets home. The smell might be bad for him so we'll need to keep the sitting-room door shut and the windows open.'

'Mum,' I said, 'did you know that Dad's already inviting all our neighbours to a party?'

'Isn't that just like the man?' said Mum, not exasperated, but brimming with enthusiastic pride.

So I went back to work without even a cup of coffee, and while I painted I listened to Dad, who had joined Mum in the kitchen, telling her what a decent chap Bob Parker seemed to be. I shuddered all over again at the scene in the front garden. If I had kids when I grew up, I'd never, never, *never* make myself look silly in front of them.

And I would also never force them to attend ethnic get-togethers. Dad was now saying to Mum that surely they could manage a bit of a hooley next Saturday and Mum was wondering whether to have a buffet or just nibbles, and would Grannie come and bring one of her trifles?

I sighed. I couldn't suggest going to stay the night with Debs or Clary, my usual escape from Mum and Dad's Celtic flings, because they'd be really hurt if I missed the first party in our new home. So I'd be trapped. It's not exactly that I'm ashamed of my proud Scottish heritage, it's just that I get tired of bevvied-up adults going into raptures over Nairn's playing and then weeping into their glasses over some Robbie Burns lyric. And I wouldn't even be able to sneak out into the woods in case I ran into the boy from the bridge – or was he the boy from the crumbling castle?

I still couldn't decide if I'd really seen someone at the

window. Perhaps he had a mad relative locked in the attic? Or perhaps I'd imagined the whole thing and he really lived in a normal brick house further over the hill.

'And if Callum can come with his accordion, we'll have a rare do!' Dad was saying.

I'd had enough. 'And so what's the story with the new shelves?' I called through innocently.

'Your Dad had this great idea that if he put his old leather-bound books in the bedroom they'd fit in fine with my four-poster effect, make it look more Victorian, and then I can add these antiqued brass light fittings from B & Q and it'll be like something from a country house!'

I sighed again and got back to work.

After a bit, when things had gone quiet, I decided to sneak into the kitchen for coffee and a bikkie. I pushed the door open and saw Mum standing at the window regarding a fan of shade cards with such a sorrowful look that I hesitated.

Dad, who'd been taking a beer from the fridge, also saw her expression, and crossed the floor to her side.

'Och, Tasha,' he said, 'you know it's not too late.'

'Heaven's sakes, Davie, of course it's too late, we're here now!'

'No, I meant it's not too late for you—'

'I wasn't thinking about that at all,' said Mum swiftly and firmly, putting the cards in her pocket. 'I was just hoping that things work out here.'

'Of course they will, we'll have a grand time!' said Dad, optimistic to the end.

'It just still feels a bit strange.' And Mum leaned back against him in a trusting way which made me feel suddenly envious and alone. Then Dad put his arms around her and, as they hadn't seen me, I crept out of the room.

CHAPTER seven

By the end of the following week my entire family was in party overdrive. Mum had finished the sitting room, Dad had invited all our new neighbours plus his old folkster pals, while Nairn and Gavin were polishing up a duet. And finally, Dad, who unlike the boys is possibly the worst Scots fiddler in the entire world, and his accordionist buddy, Callum, were planning which dance tunes to play to bring the party to a rousing finish.

As these preparations built up around me I wished, yet again, that my parents could have quiet dinner parties like Clary's family. Or if they simply had to get drunk and dance and sing, why couldn't they stick to old rockers like Rod Stewart?

So by Saturday evening I never wanted to hear the words 'Famous Grouse', 'Strip the Willow', or 'shortbread fingers' ever again. Yet there I was, arranging defrosted raspberries over sherry-soaked sponge cake, while Nairn and Gavin, and his new friends Karen and Ed, all dangerously high on sheer excitement, ran around the sitting room pinning up festoons made from tartan wrapping paper. Mum was absolutely determined that our neighbours were going to be knocked out by this old-time hanselling.

And talking of neighbours, an odd thing was that I hadn't seen the boy all week, either on the bus or anywhere in the wood. He had simply disappeared. Perhaps if I went to look for the old house, it would've gone too.

'Rosa, you're not changed yet!' Nairn had appeared in the kitchen doorway, his mates around him.

'Who says I'm getting changed?'

'But it's a *party*!' Four wee faces regarded me with disbelief and horror. 'You've got to get changed for a *party*, Rosa!'

I looked at them. Nairn and Gavin were unbearably cute in kilts and white shirts, Karen wore a glitzy green dress which set off her red hair, and Ed was wearing pristine trainers and sports gear.

'But I'm just going to be in the kitchen, doing food and stuff,' I said. 'It doesn't matter what I wear.'

'It does so matter!' Nairn was thoroughly enjoying being shocked. 'Mum! Rosa says she's not going to change!'

'Rosa!' Mum came scuttling out of the sitting room, where Dad and Callum, a big, timid, middle-aged bachelor with wild fleecy hair and a wilder Aran jumper, were unpacking instruments and pouring themselves the first pints of the evening. 'Rosa, you're not wearing old jeans and thon manky sweater!'

Mum, needless to say, was dressed glamorously in a

shiny black sequinned top and skirt, with a tartan ribbon in her hair.

'But I'll just be in the kitchen,' I repeated, clinging obstinately to my Cinderella role.

'You will not. I want you to hand round the food.'

Before I could reply to this, Grannie appeared on the scene, wearing a nifty striped polyester number, a pink cardigan and enormous diamanté earrings.

'Heaven's sakes, lassie, are you not dressed yet? That's not what you're wearing to the party, is it?'

Now that Mum, Grannie and the four kids were lined up in front of me like a firing squad, there didn't seem much point in resisting, so I pushed my way through them and stamped upstairs to my room.

I still hadn't unpacked properly, so I had to dig around until I found the dress that Mum had insisted on buying me during the summer. It was a strappy, button-through affair, and when I discovered that the top buttons no longer wanted to meet, I just crammed myself into it, achieving an effect which Debs would've envied. Then I did up my hair more carefully than usual and put on a dash of mascara and some lipstick. If Mum wanted a dolled-up daughter, that's what she was going to get.

When I came downstairs again, Mum and Grannie went into raptures over my improved appearance.

'You can look right bonny when you try,' was Grannie's comment, while Mum whisked me back upstairs for what she described scarily as a 'finishing touch'. I was all ready to resist her tartan-ribbon-poodle look, so when she produced a white silk rose and pinned it on my hair, I was so relieved that I let her get away with it.

'*The little white rose of Scotland*,' she said mistily, quoting another of Dad's favourite poems.

'Yeah, Mum,' I said. Every one of Dad's friends was now going to quote that at me. Every one, that is, except those who were going to ask me if I didn't sing or do Highland dancing or play the fiddle.

I knew better than to say anything, but when Mum had raced back to the hall, summoned by Nairn's cry that the Parkers were coming, I sat down heavily on my bed. I wondered what the tarot would have to say about the party. Since it had answered my last question with the Death card, I hadn't dared look at the pack again, but on the other hand I still hadn't returned it to Mum's room. I'd unwrapped the cards a couple of times, and they'd just felt so at home in my hands that I couldn't bear to put them back. I knew that their truth-telling might be dangerous, but it was this very danger that attracted me. Surely there wouldn't be any harm in just glancing at one card before the party? But what if I drew something terrible – the Ten of Swords, or the Five of Pentangles, which showed ragged beggars limping through the snow? That would hardly be a good omen for the evening. But I wasn't *expecting* to enjoy myself, was I? So a bad omen wouldn't make the least bit of difference.

I jumped up, retrieved the bag from behind the folders and slipped out the cards. Then, without bothering to sit down, I unwrapped them, shuffled and turned over the topmost card, whispering, 'Tell me what's going to happen tonight.'

When I saw what I was holding, I did sit down. The Two of Cups. A handsome young couple regarding one another intently while drinking from ornate goblets. Impossible. The magic had failed me. It was obvious what the card meant, but the tarot was mistaken in giving it to me. It would take more than a spell to transform any of tonight's guests into an attractive and available guy – or me into a beautiful heroine.

CHAPTER eight

My prediction rather than the tarot's had come true. Apart from the kids and myself, no one at the party was under thirty-five. The youngest of the guests were the Parkers, who, like the rest of our new neighbours, began the evening by being totally confused; however, after a drink or two they were all taking the folk singing and fiddle playing in their stride. By the time we'd reached Nairn and Gavin's performance of a set of old Scots reels I'd had enough so, wrapping myself in Grannie's cardigan, which she'd left in the kitchen, I sneaked a glass of wine and crept out the back door.

No one had drawn the curtains, so I could see through the kitchen to the living room, where the two boys stood, violins raised. Everyone had gone quiet. I hate to admit it, but as I listened in the moonlit garden, my throat ached and my eyes felt hot. I wasn't going to cry at a Scots fiddle tune. I wasn't going to be so old-fashioned and sentimental. I sniffed back my tears and took a sip of the wine, glad when the set came to an end and the boys bowed to the applauding guests. But then Gavin stepped back and Nairn began to play alone. He really is good for a wee boy, and the piece he'd chosen, 'The Rowan Tree', had a sad lilt to it that would have broken a much harder heart than mine.

I turned round and marched down the path towards the woods before the mascara began to actually drip down my cheeks. A little more wine, a stroll under the trees and I could return to my waitress duties without damp eyes and a telltale pink face.

As I opened the gate, someone who had also been listening detached himself from the darkness.

'Your brother's a good little player,' he said.

I stood there, one hand on the latch, my glass in the other, glad that my face was in the shadows. After our two previous encounters I certainly wasn't going to let myself down by appearing startled.

'So how do you know he's my brother?' I said, with what I hoped was disdain.

'I've seen him through the window.'

So I'd been right when I'd said that anyone could see us from the woods! Just like in a movie, someone *had* been watching us.

'I always go home this way, so I can't help but see in,' the boy continued, without a hint of apology. 'You really ought to draw the curtains.'

'So I suppose you're on your way home now,' I said sarcastically.

'Yes, I am, actually. Last bus. I didn't know your people were having a party.'

People! Not family or folks or parents, but people! I

shouldn't have been taken aback by his posh accent, having seen him in his school blazer, but his upper-class voice, along with his casual attitude towards watching us, as though we were a mildly amusing sitcom, infuriated me.

'I do hope you're finding our old folk customs entertaining,' I said. 'We'll be dancing next if you want to stay and watch that.'

'I'm sorry,' he said, in a very slightly more normal voice. 'I didn't mean to spy on you. I just stopped to listen to your brother. He's really good.'

'Yes, he is,' I agreed, less angrily.

'I bet you get tired of hearing people say that.'

I almost found myself smiling. 'Have you got a talented little brother or sister?'

'No, I just guessed.'

'So do you play the violin then?'

'Certainly not.' He was actually smiling. 'Here.' He rummaged in his pocket, pulled out a crumpled packet of Gauloises and offered me one. 'Do you smoke?'

'Certainly not,' I echoed.

'Sticking to the bevvy?'

'Have some.' I held out the glass. He hesitated, probably not wanting to touch something I'd sullied with my lipsticky, schemie lips, but after he'd lit his cigarette he reached out his free hand, took the glass and drank.

'That's good stuff.' He sounded a bit surprised.

I don't know anything about wine because Dad's a beer and whisky drinker and Mum prefers drinks that end in an 'i' like Martini or Bacardi. This was a bottle the Mowats, an elderly couple from the end of the row, had brought, but I wasn't going to betray our uncouth tastes.

'Nothing but the best for the McBrides,' I said.

'That's your name?'

It may not be the classiest of names, but nothing to be ashamed of. 'Yes. Rosaleen McBride.'

Then, to my complete astonishment, he said, 'That's a beautiful name.'

I wondered if he were teasing, but he looked, as far as I could see by the moonlight, perfectly serious.

'Makes you sound like a gypsy.'

'Rosaleen's Irish – I mean, I'm not Irish, but it's from a favourite song of Mum's. I've always thought it was a bit over the top. I'm usually just called Rosa.' For some reason I was now starting to gush like Debs. If I didn't watch it, I'd be batting my eyelashes next.

'I think it's very romantic, being called after a song. I'm Andy, Andy Byron.'

'What!' I exclaimed. 'Like the poet?'

'So you've heard of him?'

'Of *course* I've heard of Byron!' Dad is an English teacher, after all, and although I hadn't read anything by the famous poet, I certainly knew his name.

'Sorry, sorry,' said Andy, waving his glowing cigarette dramatically before taking another drag. 'Not everyone has. And no, I'm no relation.'

'*I* think it's very romantic to have the same name as a poet,' I said, 'although I suppose it must be as annoying for you as having a cute wee brother is for me.'

'Is it so very annoying?'

We both turned towards the window, where, glamorously back-lit, Nairn was bowing to his rapturous fans.

'Kind of – I mean, not really. I'm proud of him and all that, it's just that he's good at *everything*.'

'So what are you good at?' Andy handed me back the glass, and for a moment our fingers touched on the stem.

I repressed a little shiver. 'Oh, not much,' I said casually, taking a quick sip of wine. 'I'm doing a couple of sciences – and I do know a lot about films. My friend Clary and I won a movie-trivia quiz last summer.'

Andy laughed. 'Two sciences! I'm impressed. They only let me do one. But the movie quiz – that really is something!'

I laughed too, but I wished I hadn't mentioned Clary. She was actually much more like Andy than I was – posh parents, big house, although her home was a Victorian semi, not a crumbling mansion. If that was where Andy lived.

'Actually,' I said, as lightly as possible, 'actually, I shouldn't have been mad at you for looking at our house. When I saw you last Saturday, I'd just been looking at yours – I mean, that house just beyond the trees, that is where you live, isn't it?'

Andy gave a sort of cross, amused sigh. 'What do *you* think?'

'Well, that's the direction you were going in, and there don't seem to be any other houses – it's just that it's . . . it looks like a—'

'Ruin, I think, is the word you're looking for.' He'd gone back to being distant and posh again.

'No, no,' I said desperately. 'I thought it was beautiful, really. It's just there was so much ivy growing over it and everything . . .' My words faded away.

'You thought it could've been haunted, I suppose.'

'*No*, of course not.' I remembered the face at the window. 'So your family *do* live there?'

'Yes. Christabel – that's my mother – and I. Just the two of us. Cosy.'

'Oh,' I said. 'Cosy' certainly wasn't the word I would've used. And so that face at the window must've been his mother!

'The two remaining Byrons in our historic home. Well, my father's historic home, actually, but we're the two remaining inhabitants.'

'Oh,' I said again, and then, when he didn't elaborate, I held out the glass to him. 'Go on, finish it.'

'Don't you want it?'

'No, I don't really like it. I was just drinking it to help me through the party.'

'Weren't you enjoying yourself?'

'I *hate* my parents' parties!' I was surprised at my own vehemence. 'Everyone gets drunk and Mum sings "My Love Is Like a Red, Red Rose" and Dad plays the fiddle – he's nothing like as good as Nairn – it's just so embarrassing. And I'm supposed to join in.'

Andy finished off my wine. 'It sounds fantastic. Perhaps you'll invite me to the next one.'

I felt hot and confused and flattered. Of course he didn't mean it. He was definitely teasing this time.

'Dad invited everyone for miles around,' I said. 'If he'd known you were there, he'd have invited you and your mother as well.'

'Oh, but nobody knows we're there. That's the beauty of Drumglass, we never get callers.'

I could understand that.

'However, next time you're having a nature ramble, you might knock on the door.'

I felt even hotter, and my skin prickled against Grannie's cardigan. Thank goodness it was too dark for him to see either my red face or the lurid pink of the woolly.

Then he handed back the glass, and our fingers touched again. 'Thanks for the drink.'

He hadn't given me time to find out if it were a real invitation.

'It was a pleasure,' I said.

'I'll see you around then.'

'Yes,' I said inadequately. I wished I could make some seductive remark like Debs would've done, but instead I found myself saying, 'I'd better go in now. I'm supposed to be handing round food.'

'Time I was off too. See you then. Goodnight.'

And then he was gone, just gone, vanished into the trees, nothing left of him but a trace of French tobacco smoke.

'Andy Byron,' I whispered. 'No relation to the poet.'

Had he really been there? Would I ever see him again? I looked down at the glass in my hand. It was a heavy, cut-glass affair, part of a set that Mum and Dad had been given as a wedding present. Almost a goblet, in fact. I held it up to the moonlight, the glittering facets reminding me of something I'd seen very recently – the goblets from which the lovers were drinking in the Two of Cups!

Although nobody could see me, I went on turning the glass between my hands to hide my shock.

In the end it was the tarot's prediction, and not mine, that had come true.

CHAPTER nine

'So how was the party?' Debs, her curls frizzed up into a topknot, and wearing, despite the chilly autumn wind, a tiny T-shirt, was condescending to speak to me for the first time in a couple of days. Ever since the weekend she'd been draped over Franklin, and the only reason she'd peeled herself away from him now was that we were going to biology, which wasn't on the thicko hulk's timetable.

'Not so bad,' I replied coolly. I was a bit miffed that she had taken so long to ask, and I certainly wasn't going to fill her in on the enticing details of my encounter in the woods. Even the party had been all right after that.

When I'd got back to the house, dizzy with wine and surprise, the house-warming was in full swing. I'd intended creeping upstairs to brood over my meeting with the mysterious Andy Byron, but I'd been seized by Mr Mowat, who wanted a partner for the Eightsome Reel. It would've been too rude to refuse this chivalrous old man, so I'd squeezed in beside him – there was just room for one set – and in a moment we were whirling around, and I discovered that I was actually enjoying myself. Mr Mowat was an excellent dancer, and between us we got everyone to do all the figures correctly. Then I danced it all over again with Mr Parker, shoving him into place when he tried to go the wrong way in the Grand Chain, and finally, before I knew it, Mum and I were singing 'Ye Banks and Braes o' Bonny Doon', something I hadn't done in public since I was Nairn's age. I knew that I was making a fool of myself, but it was almost worth it to see Mum and Dad looking so proud and happy.

I meant to tell Debs all this, but before I could begin she asked what was, for her, the vital question.

'Any talent?'

I shook my head decisively. 'Nah.'

'Too bad.' She blew a kiss to Franklin, who was lumbering off in the direction of the PE department. 'He is so sexy. It's the accent.'

Oh yeah? I said to myself as I dug around in my bag for my science books.

'What's that then?' With the disappearance of her idol, Debs had returned to being her old sharp self. She tugged something out of my open bag – the tarot book. Since my amazing success as a fortune-teller on Saturday night, all my scruples had fallen away, and I'd been studying the cards every spare minute. Of course, I hadn't brought the actual cards to school, but I'd been reading the book on the bus.

'The tarot?' Debs voice was a squeak of awed surprise. 'I didn't know you could read the tarot, Rosie.'

'I can't,' I said. 'At least, not yet.' I looked on helplessly as Debs riffled through my precious book.

'Have you got a pack then?'

'Well, yes,' I admitted.

'Oh, Rosie, tell my fortune! Come back to mine after school and reveal what the future holds in store!'

There was no doubt what she *wanted* it to hold in store. In fact, it would be dead easy to make up a fortune for Debs because I knew her so well, but it would probably be against some sort of psychic ethics.

'I've told you, I don't know how to do it. And, anyway, I haven't got the cards with me.'

'Bring them on Friday afternoon, we'll do it then.'

Friday afternoon is a holiday in our school. We're supposed to engage in cultural activities, but actually all the girls go downtown to buy new lipsticks and clothes for the weekend, while the boys hang out in Virgin or PC World.

'But I don't know how, Debs, I'm just beginning!'

'Leanne, look what Rosie's got, she's going to tell my fortune on Friday afternoon – why don't you and Marisa come too?'

This was getting out of control. Leanne and Marisa, two of those girls who have to be best friends because they look exactly alike, had wandered up, drawn by Debs's squeals. Now they stood looking over her shoulder at my book, their long tails of blonde hair flapping in the breeze.

'Can you really tell fortunes, Rosa?' said Leanne.

It was no use. No one would believe me when I said I couldn't, so I might as well agree. It would be good practice to try some actual spreads, and it would just be in fun.

'All right then, I'll bring the cards on Friday,' I said.

'Great!' cried Debs.

'I've always wanted to go to a fortune-teller,' said Marisa, 'but Mum wouldn't let me. She disapproves of it.'

I felt a horrible twinge of guilt when Marisa said this. Mum had been so upset when I'd found the cards, and I knew perfectly well that if she had even a suspicion of what I was up to, she'd go mental. I opened my mouth to say it was all a mistake – but then I saw the expressions on the three faces turned towards me. Debs, Marisa and Leanne were regarding me with a mixture of excitement and, yes, respect, which I'd never received from them before.

OK then. If they were such tattie-heads as to believe I was a real fortune-teller, it was their look out. I would teach myself one of the easier spreads before Friday, and trust to luck for the rest.

Then I saw Clary approaching across the playground. She was actually reading as she walked, but owing to some special Clary magic, she was managing to avoid all the games of football without once glancing up from the page. As she came closer, I began to feel as though I were at the centre of some symbolic struggle between Good and Evil. There were Debs, Marisa and Leanne on the one side, like the three witches in *Macbeth*, and on the other there was Clary in her long velvet skirt, an angel unsullied by even the touch of a muddy football.

I grabbed my book back from Debs and stuffed it into my bag as Clary came up to us.

'OK, Friday,' Debs said. 'Remember, you promised, Rosie.'

'What's happening on Friday?' Clary looked up.

The others were all watching me. None of them like Clary, whom they consider stuck-up.

I fumbled with the catch on my bag. 'I'm going round to Debs's to collect some knitting patterns which her mum has for my mum,' I said. 'She's making some stuff for the autumn fair.'

It was a feeble sort of answer, but so boring that Clary accepted it with a quiet sniff and went on reading. She doesn't like Debs and the others any more than they like her and she can never understand why I hang out with them. But Debs and I grew up on the same street, and we used to play on the swings and go guising together and all that other little-kid stuff.

Anyway, I didn't say any more, but I felt really bad inside. I knew that I was doing something neither Mum nor Clary would approve of, and I was almost angry with Clary for not realizing this and doing something to stop me.

I missed the early bus again that evening because I'd had to stay on after school to discuss my English project, an essay on that gloomy rural epic *Tess of the D'Urbervilles*. When another bus eventually arrived I climbed aboard, took a quick look at the lower deck, went upstairs, took another look along the rows of commuters and then slumped down in the nearest seat. Not a trace of a tall dark figure in a daft blazer. As I'd never seen Andy on the early bus, I'd thought he might be on this one – not that I really cared, of course. Just because I'd last met him in romantic circumstances, it didn't mean that I was going to start behaving like Debs, all giggly and girlish. In fact, I've never been like that about a boy. I know all the guys at our school too well. After years and years together at primary and then high school, they just seemed like mildly irritating brothers.

But Andy was different. And not just different, but mysterious. How did he come to live in what looked like a ruin, yet go to such a grand school? And did he have a girl-friend to match the school? I'd been wondering this several times a day since Saturday, and by now I could picture her quite clearly. She'd have an English accent and long, straight, naturally blonde hair and she'd be tall and slim – the exact opposite to me, in fact.

Yet he *had* said he'd see me again. Had he really meant it?

In order to stop my thoughts from trailing around in these boring and pathetic circles, I pulled out the tarot book, but it fell open at the page I'd been reading most often – the description of the Two of Cups, the card I'd drawn on Saturday night: 'This card indicates mutual love, and the beginning of a romantic love affair.'

'Is that the sort of thing they teach at your school?'

I slammed the book shut, praying that he hadn't seen the page I'd been looking at.

'Of course not,' I said. 'I was just interested.'

'It's all rubbish,' Andy said, unconsciously echoing Mum and Clary. He sat down beside me. 'OK if I sit here?'

A minute ago I'd been longing to see him, but now that

he'd appeared at my side, doing that irritating thing of asking if it was all right to do something he'd already done, I felt really nippy.

'No,' I said. 'I mean, fine. Actually, my mum would agree with you. She thinks all fortune-telling's stupid.'

'Now my mother's the direct opposite. She's quite into the tarot.'

'Is she really?' I was astonished. I'd been imagining Andy's mother as a country version of Gavin's mum, a woman in a floral cotton blouse and a tweed skirt who was frightfully keen on her garden. Now I wondered if I'd ever get to know Andy well enough to meet his mother and have the opportunity of asking her advice about the cards. Immediately I thought, How awful if he thinks I want to get to know him better for *any* reason, so I added quickly, 'I'm not *terribly* interested, but I found a pack knocking about at home so I just thought I'd find out a bit more.'

'Knocking about?' Andy wrinkled up his long face, which was too much like that of some very intelligent animal to be completely handsome. 'Christabel would faint if she could hear you. The tarot pack has to be kept wrapped in silk and treated with all the respect due to a sacred object. According to her, that is.'

'This pack's wrapped up,' I said, only now understanding why. 'No one's touched it for years.'

'Who does it belong to then? No one's supposed to touch a tarot pack apart from its owner.'

I glanced at him uncertainly, and despite his look of faint boredom, as though this entire conversation were beneath him, I so much wanted to discuss this with someone that I said cautiously, 'I don't really know who they belonged to. Some old auntie of Mum's, I suppose.'

'But you don't know for sure?' Andy was suddenly paying more attention to what I was saying.

'No. Why should I?'

'Only, like I said, you shouldn't touch someone else's cards.'

'Why not?'

'Oh, some magic guff about disturbing vibrations.'

'I've never heard that before,' I said huffily. I certainly wasn't going to let Andy Byron lay down the law to me, although I was feeling more and more uneasy.

'OK, OK,' he said. 'I know it's none of my business – I just don't think you should play about with them.'

I turned right round and glared at him. 'I'm not playing about!'

'You have to take them seriously, that's what Christabel says.'

'Who says I'm not serious?'

'You did. You said you weren't terribly interested.'

'Well, perhaps I *am* interested but I didn't want to say so to somebody I hardly know!'

We were both quiet for a moment, our bodies touching on the narrow seat.

Andy gave in first. 'Sorry,' he said, holding up both his hands. 'You needn't get angry with me. It's just that Christabel said it could be unlucky. Using someone else's cards.'

I hesitated. The cards didn't *feel* unlucky; in fact, it was the exact opposite. I remembered how, when I'd found the bag, it seemed as though it *wanted* me to open it; how the cards had *wanted* me to hold them, but now, after what Andy had said, these feelings seemed fanciful, and even dangerous.

And when I thought about it – look what the cards had already made me do! I'd stolen them from Mum, lied to Clary, and I was intending to cheat Debs and the others with a load of made-up fortunes! And, worst of all, I'd concealed from Andy, my new friend, that the cards actually belonged to Mum.

'And especially when, for all you know, the owner might be dead,' continued Andy, when I remained silent.

I concealed my shiver with a cross shrug of my shoulders. 'What possible difference could that make?'

'Well, cards have to be passed on from one owner to another. You can't just throw them out; the old owner has to give the new owner permission to use them.'

Sitting there on the steamy bus, a huge light was dawning. I'd seen by her face that Mum, for some weird reason, was almost *afraid* of the cards, and now I understood why, despite that, she'd had to keep them. She couldn't take the risk of chucking them out and attracting some mysterious ill-fortune.

However, I wouldn't give Andy the satisfaction of knowing that he'd scared me.

'That doesn't worry me,' I said firmly. 'That's all just superstition.'

But I didn't believe my own words. After Friday I really would return the cards to their hiding place.

'Fine,' said Andy, settling himself still further down into the seat. 'It's your funeral.' There was a second's uneasy silence. 'Sorry. I didn't mean that.'

But perhaps it was what he was actually thinking? I've often noticed how *my* real thoughts are inclined to slip out if I don't watch what I'm saying.

'No, I didn't. Really,' he repeated.

'OK,' I said, and I turned round and stared out the window, as though the passing suburbs were as fascinating as some exotic foreign city. However, with every row of bungalows, every garden of privet and conifer, I was aware of precious minutes slipping past, minutes during which I could've been captivating Andy with my wit and charm. I could've been showing him that although I wasn't tall and slim and blonde I had all sorts of other desirable qualities.

Such as? I asked myself cynically. Not too bad looking, in a curvy, brunette sort of way; fairly intelligent, halfway through *Tess of the D'Urbervilles* – was that enough to make Andy Byron, clever, presumably wealthy and very nearly handsome, interested in me?

Seriously unlikely.

'I'm getting off at the next stop. Got to pick up some stuff.'

The journey was almost over, and I'd barely said a civil word, far less a fascinating one! And now Andy was getting to his feet, hoisting his bag to his shoulder.

'Mine's the one after,' I said, consciousness of the missed

opportunity washing over me in a big, regretful wave.

'No, get off here and I'll walk you up the hill. That bit of road's terribly dark.'

Andy was right. Because I'd missed the earlier bus again, it was now darker than usual. 'All right,' I muttered ungraciously and, gathering up my stuff, I followed him down the stairs and off the bus.

'Just a few oddments,' he said, heading for the small square of shops which, set around a tired shrub or two, were our suburb's idea of a mall. Like all open spaces in Edinburgh, it was sliced across by a bitter wind which blew straight from the bleak hills and the cold North Sea.

'Whoever designed this place obviously didn't live here,' I said, as we scuttled into the supermarket.

'No one *lives* here,' said Andy; 'just *exists*. I mean, sorry, Rosa, I know you've just arrived, but this really is the ends of the earth. Teuchterland.'

'I didn't *choose* to come here,' I said. 'We moved because my little brother's got asthma. What's your excuse?'

Andy was looking up and down the aisles, as though in search of rare foodstuffs beyond the scope of the suburban store.

'We have the house,' he said dismissively, waving one thin hand.

How could I forget the house, huddled down in the woods, creeper-covered, like something from a horror movie?

'But do you have to live there?' For all I despised our brick box, it had to be a hundred times more comfortable than the ruin Andy called home.

'Yes,' he said shortly. 'Where have they put the cereals? Always moving stuff around.'

Obviously close of conversation.

While we'd been talking Andy had been filling his wire basket, picking out items unhesitatingly.

'Doesn't your mum do the shopping with the car?' That seemed a safe enough question.

'We don't have a car.'

I hadn't made things any better. So, despite his grand accent, Andy not only lived in a ruin, he didn't have a car. I thought of asking why his mother didn't just walk down to the supermarket but, as Andy was looking more and more remote, I decided to shut up before he regretted his offer to walk me home. Instead, I trotted along behind him, reflecting that if he looked like a noble and intelligent animal – a collie, say – then I probably resembled some sort of terrier with my curly hair straggling into my eyes.

Then, as I silently pattered, I couldn't help but notice how basic Andy's shopping was compared to ours. I'd never thought of my family as being extravagant, but when Mum brings home the weekly shopping, there are always loads of goodies – Häagen Dazs, chocolate biscuits, stuff from the deli counter. Andy, however, was piling his basket with own-brand cornflakes, margarine and economy Cheddar. The only luxury product was a packet of expensive Italian coffee.

'Who's the caffeine freak?' I said, to break the silence.

'Christabel. She lives on the stuff. Terribly bad for you.'

'Really?' Not nearly as bad as smoking, I almost said, but had the sense to keep quiet.

'If you've got nerves like hers.'

We had reached the checkout, so after he'd paid we headed back into the cold and windy darkness. It *was* nicer having company. Even Andy, who could be so rude, and seemed so easily offended.

'I don't like coming here in the dark,' I admitted.

'I'm surprised your parents let you.'

'I'm usually back on the early bus. And Mum would meet me, but she'd either have to bring Nairn, or find someone to leave him with.'

'The brother with asthma?'

'More a suspicion of asthma.'

'Do I get the impression that little brother and his asthma come first with Mummy and Daddy?'

It was scary but oddly comforting to have someone say this horrible, guilty thought out loud.

'He did get really bad when the traffic was re-routed past our old flat,' I said quickly. It seemed very important to push down all the dark, ugly thoughts which were rising at the back of my head, like dinosaurs hauling themselves out of a swamp.

'And so you had to move, no matter how you felt about it?'

'Yes,' I said. This was the first time that anyone had taken my regret about the move seriously, and as he spoke, a very curious feeling began to creep over me. Did this odd, standoffish stranger understand me better than my own family and my best friend? I glanced at his dark silhouette as he paced along beside me, seemingly not bothered by the weight of his bag.

'Come on, there's a short cut here.' Andy turned abruptly off the pavement and disappeared into the rustling undergrowth.

'Are you sure?' I stopped, all my fears of the dark returning. Out here on the hillside, the country was reasserting itself with bramble tripwires and patches of menacing shadow. I could smell the river.

'Yes, it cuts off the corner. I always come this way. I told you.'

So that explained why I'd never seen him on the road, and also why he'd seen us through the kitchen window.

'This way.' Andy was already climbing between the trees, so I followed him, stepping bravely onto the crackly, leafy ground.

'Here, just this steep bit.' Andy leaned back, took my hand, pulled me up behind him and then let go and went on walking. I followed him, not just breathless from the climb, but because I seemed to be having difficulty breathing in a calm, normal fashion. Also my *hand* actually felt odd, as though it ought still to be grasping something and was now cold and lonely.

'And here you are!'

The path had twisted round a final clump of brambles and come out at the back gate, just at the spot where we'd met during Nairn's violin solo.

'I didn't know there was another path here,' I said brightly. If he could sound normal after holding my hand for that long moment, then so could I. 'I'd better go in. Mum'll be worrying.'

I opened the gate and stepped briskly into the garden. I certainly wasn't going to hang around looking as though I hoped he'd say something about seeing me again.

However, as the gate shut between us, he put his hand on it next to mine but not quite touching, and said, 'If you want to ask Christabel about the tarot you could come over on Saturday afternoon.'

'Could I really?' I was horrified to hear myself sounding eager and excited, rather than sophisticated and cool, like the girls I imagined he knew.

'Sure. Why not?'

Why not? Because it seemed too good to be true that he'd asked me! I took a deep breath and said as casually as possible. 'Thanks, I'd like to.'

'OK then. About two thirty?'

'Do I just go up to the front door or what?' I'd suddenly imagined myself going around and around his house, trying to find a way in.

Andy laughed. 'It's not so *very* forbidding. Tell you what I'll meet you in the wood on top of the hill.'

'All right. See you there.'

'See you.'

And we both turned away, Andy melting into the woods and me walking towards the red, red brick of home.

CHAPTER ten

After school on Friday the three others and I took off for Debs's place. Really annoyingly, Debs and Leanne carried on as though we were doing some big secret thing we didn't want anyone to know about, with lots of girly whispering and giggling, which, of course, had the exact opposite effect. By the time we got out of the school gate, all the other girls in the class knew that we were doing something mysterious from which they were excluded, and I saw Clary giving me a hurt and disdainful look before she walked off in the opposite direction.

Debs's mum's flat was only a few streets from the school, so after we'd bought ourselves sandwiches and crisps from the deli, we went straight round and Debs let us into the stair. As we climbed up to the first floor, she said. 'Hurry, Rosie, I can hardly wait. We'll do it once we've had our rolls – we'll pull the curtains and light candles, like a proper fortune-teller's.'

We followed Debs into the kitchen – her mum was at work – and while Debs made us teas and coffees and we ate our lunch, there was a lot of gossip about amazing predictions which friends or relations had received, all of which made me feel even worse about the afternoon ahead. I couldn't possibly predict anything! I had taught myself to lay out one of the easier spreads, the Celtic Cross, and I'd gone over and over the cards, but if I came up with something heavy like Death or the Ten of Swords, how would I explain it away?

The others, obviously, didn't share my fears, so after scoffing their rolls they hustled me into the sitting room. Debs pulled the curtains, as she'd threatened, and lit some candles, and the girls settled themselves on the squashy sofa and chairs, while I sat down cross-legged on the carpet and prepared to lay out the cards. The others had fallen silent – an incredible feat – and this made me even more nervous. Why on earth had I let myself in for this? But I was sure of one thing: this might be my first appearance as a fortune-teller, but it would also be my last. Mum, Clary *and* Andy couldn't all be wrong – and especially Andy, whose mother was an expert.

So, taking a deep breath, I shuffled the cards and handed them to Debs. After she'd cut the pack, I laid out the top-most ten cards in a cross and turned them over. As they flipped onto the silk square, I breathed out in relief. Nothing terrible here. Mind you, there was no sign that Debs and Franklin were going to settle down and live happily ever after, but a card promising travel was there, something Debs has always wanted to do, and, just as I'd suspected, I was able to weave a perfectly credible fortune out of what I already knew about her, and what I'd managed to learn about the cards.

'Oh, Rosie, that is just plain *amazing*,' she said when I'd finished. 'How did you *know* all that?'

Simple, you daft bisom, I thought. Anybody who'd met Debs for five minutes would have known exactly what she was like and exactly what she wanted, and I'd had the advantage of knowing her for *years*.

Marisa and Leanne were equally impressed.

'But how did you *do* it, Rosa?' said Leanne, leaning forwards, her face a pale oval in the candlelight. 'All that stuff you said about Debs's ambitions was dead true. She was just saying the other day that she wanted to work in the holiday business.'

'OK, Leanne, I'll do yours next,' I said, gathering up Mum's worn old cards with a professional snap. I was getting into this. If I could keep my head, and if nothing tricky came up, I might just get through the readings without an absolute disaster.

'No, Marisa, you go first,' said Leanne unselfishly, so Marisa shuffled and cut and I dealt and turned the cards. Her spread was less obvious than Debs's, partly because I don't know Marisa so well, and partly because some of the cards were more obscure. However, I looked at them in a wise, considering sort of way before launching into a spiel based around the two central cards which showed a woman alone in a garden being crossed by a gloomy father figure, the Emperor.

'This first card shows that you're feeling isolated at the

moment, but you're putting the time to good use by being extra creative' – it seemed safe to say this, as Marisa, like Mum, is brilliant at art and sewing and stuff – 'but your progress is being blocked by this older man.'

Somehow, once I'd started, the words flowed faster and faster, although what I was saying didn't seem to be making much sense. All I knew about Marisa's home life was that her parents were divorced and her mum had married again. However, all the cards seemed to point to a troubled present, but a future in which Marisa, if she listened to her intuition, would find happiness through being with children.

While I said all this, Marisa remained disappointingly silent, and when I'd finished, all she said was, 'Yes, I'd quite like to work with kids.'

I decided that I'd probably got everything else wrong and she was too tactful to say so, but Leanne immediately jumped in, demanding her turn.

Leanne's spread, by contrast, was more like Debs's – very upbeat, with lots of happy families and romance, although the romance was not for Leanne herself, but for someone in her family.

'I can see a wedding,' I announced. 'Not yours, but some-one very close to you, probably a member of your family.' As I spoke, a picture came into my head of Leanne in a fluffy bridesmaid's dress, with roses woven through her pale blonde hair. It was absolutely irrational, but there they were, two Leannes: the real one on the sofa in front of me, in jeans and wee knitted top, and the imaginary, drifting in an old-fashioned cloud of ruffled silk. 'And,' I continued firmly, prompted by the same unknown force, 'this person, a young man, will be asking you to be a bridesmaid.'

'But that can't be true!' protested Debs. 'Bruce can't be getting married, he's only seventeen!'

Bruce, Leanne's brother, had only just left school.

Leanne, however, had fallen back onto the sofa, a look of mingled astonishment and triumph on her pretty face. 'But it *is* true!' she said. 'It's all absolutely true. I *am* going to be a bridesmaid!'

I was as amazed as the others, if not actually more so. I could do this. I could really do it. When I said what the cards told me to, it wasn't nonsense that came out of my mouth, but the truth. I'd thought that I'd have to pretend to be a fortune-teller, when, in fact, I really *was* one.

Had Mum once felt like this?

While I was struggling to get my breath back without betraying the fact that I was overwhelmed by Leanne's declaration, Debs and Marisa were squealing: 'But who's getting married?'

'Why didn't you tell us?'

'It can't be Bruce!'

'Of course it's not Bruce,' said Leanne. 'It's my big brother, Pete, in London. He phoned last night to say his girlfriend's pregnant and they're going to get married. Mum's over the moon, first grandchild and all, and I'm to be chief bridesmaid! And I didn't tell anyone 'cause I wanted to see if Rosa could really see my future.'

What a cow! She'd tried to trick me, but I'd shown her what real psychic powers looked like. Well, I supposed I had. Where else could my information have come from? I'd just looked at the cards and the image of Leanne in her bridesmaid's dress had appeared before me like some sort of vision. It was actually a bit scary.

'I just don't *believe* it,' said Debs. 'You really can do it, just like a real fortune-teller.'

She sounded so surprised that I, her oldest friend, could actually do something properly, I almost felt offended.

'But how *did* you do it?' said Leanne, leaning forwards to peer at her spread.

'It's all in the cards,' I said mysteriously. 'You just need to be able to read their language.'

'You mean, like a computer code?' asked Marisa unexpectedly.

'Well, yes,' I said, struck by this new idea. It was a bit like that, but there was something more; something I couldn't explain.

'Because everything you said about my cards was true too,' said Marisa quietly. 'I want to go and live with my dad, but my stepfather won't let me, because he says it would upset Mum, and I want to train as a nursery nurse, but they want me to do business studies.'

I was, if anything, even more surprised than I had been at Leanne's revelation. I hadn't known any of that stuff about Marisa, I'd just followed the cards and the voice inside my head.

I looked at my small audience, their faces dim in the candlelight. Debs still seemed stunned, Leanne was awestruck, and Marisa actually a bit frightened. Perhaps if

I'd had any sense, I'd have been frightened too, but what I was really feeling was a tremendous buzz, a spacey, energized sensation.

'You're just as good as the woman Mum's friend went to, who told her she'd get married again and have two more children,' Debs was saying, as though in a trance. 'It really is weird.'

'Mum'll never believe me when I tell her you knew about Pete's wedding,' said Leanne. 'I mean, we only knew ourselves last night.'

I shrugged with becoming modesty and gathered up the cards.

'You know, Rosie, what you should do,' said Debs, reverting to her old pushy self. 'What you should do is a fortune-telling turn at the autumn fair.'

This is the school's annual fundraiser. There are all the usual stalls – games, teas and homebaking – with the proceeds being divided between the school and some local charity.

'You could be billed as Gypsy Rosa,' continued Debs, building up speed, 'and get all dressed up in shawls and earrings and stuff. It would be brilliant!'

'Oh yes!' said Leanne. 'You can quote me on your poster: "*Sensationally accurate*" – *Leanne Collins*.'

'Mrs Grier will love it – she's always on about how pupils should be more involved,' went on Debs, virtually bouncing with excitement.

Mrs Grier is the teacher in charge of the stalls.

'No, no, wait, I don't think so,' I said in a panic.

'Why not?' Debs, unable to keep still, had jumped up and was pulling back the curtains, while Leanne blew out the candles. Only Marisa remained silent and it occurred to me that maybe she didn't like me seeing so deeply into her private life.

'There's dozens of reasons I can't do it,' I said. 'I mean, Mum and Dad would go mental and, anyway, I couldn't keep it up for a whole afternoon.'

Now that Debs had let in the bleak, rainy daylight I was beginning to feel as though my psychic exploits had never happened.

'Don't be such a loser, Rosie,' said Debs. 'It would be totally brilliant and it's for the good of the school.'

I didn't think Debs had ever considered the good of the school before in her entire life.

'Don't be daft, Debs,' I said, with as much conviction as possible. 'It's a hopeless idea. Mrs Grier will probably just think it's tacky, and my parents would have a fit.'

In fact, Mum would have worse than a fit. She'd been angry enough when I'd discovered the pack by mistake, so I hardly dared imagine her reaction if she learned that I'd not only stolen them deliberately, but was doing readings.

'What a lovely wee bag, Rosa! Did you make it?' Marisa stretched out her hand towards the velvet.

In my alarm, I'd forgotten that Mum's name was embroidered on the bag.

'No,' I said, quickly shoving it away among my stuff. 'It was some old auntie's.' Then, before there could be any more questions from Marisa or bossing over the fair from

Debs and Leanne, I got up and went to fetch my jacket from the kitchen. 'Thanks for the coffee, Debs, I'll have to go now. Give my love to your mum.'

'Don't go, Rosie! Mum's got a great flouncy skirt you could try on for being a gypsy in.'

'Debs, I am not going to be a gypsy,' I said, from the secure retreat of my cuddly old jacket. 'And I've got to go now to catch my bus.'

'I wish you'd never moved house,' mourned Debs.

'So do I,' I said, but as I thumped my way down the stair, I realized that I didn't quite believe what I'd just said. If we hadn't moved, I would never have found the cards. And I would never have met Andy.

CHAPTER eleven

In fact, the only time I'd stopped thinking about Andy was when I was actually reading the cards. I knew I was behaving like Debs over Franklin, and I despised myself, but I couldn't help it. All the time I was sitting in class or doing my homework or munching my way through family meals. I was going over and over our previous encounters, and fantasizing about Saturday. What would his mother be like? What was his house like inside? Would he want to see me again?

All in all, I was in such a dwam, as Grannie would've said, that real life seemed to be happening very far away and immensely slowly. Inside my head, I was dashing full tilt towards Saturday afternoon, already seeing myself running up the hill and Andy coming out of the trees to meet me – but outside, lessons and journeys were carrying on at their usual pace.

Anyway, Saturday finally arrived, bringing with it a whole load of new worries, the most important of which was: how could I slip out unnoticed? I could just imagine

Dad's galumphing, heavy-handed jokes and Mum's niggling questions if they knew I was going to meet a boy. However, as so often happens, all my worrying proved to have been a complete waste of time. The moment lunch was over, my family disappeared in different directions like beads off a broken necklace. Dad and Bob Parker, already the best of buddies, settled down in front of the TV, cans at the ready, for an afternoon of dedicated sports viewing, Nairn was picked up by Ed and his dad, and Mum zipped off in the car to lay in more DIY supplies.

So, with no one taking the least interest in what I was doing, I was left with worry number two: what was I going to wear? I'd already washed and conditioned my hair into a state of unusual sleekness, and put on some mascara and a green liner that was supposed to make my eyes look more hazel than Indian tea brown. My favourite T-shirt, however, didn't exactly match all this glamour, so I decided on a little black silk jersey number that Mum had given me for my birthday, but which I'd hardly worn because it was so embarrassingly revealing. With this I wore my least tatty jeans, and I was just putting on my jacket when I realized that time, which during my girly dithering had been moving so slowly, had mysteriously speeded up, and it was now twenty-five past two.

I shoved the velvet bag into my pocket and raced out of the house. What if I were late and Andy didn't wait for me? What if he thought I wasn't coming? I was halfway up the field when it occurred to me that if Andy were in the wood he'd see me hurrying to meet him, which would be shamefully uncool, so I slowed down to a saunter. It was also beginning to strike me that this whole thing might be a terrible mistake. I couldn't be anything like the sort of girl whom Andy usually brought home. He'd probably regretted his invitation the moment he'd given it. It was the cards, I decided. He'd asked me to come for the sake of meeting his mother, not because he really wanted to see me.

By now, despite going at an absolute snail's crawl, I'd reached the edge of the straggly wood. Overwhelmed by my gloomy thoughts, I wanted to turn back, but I automatically followed the path that Andy must have made, going to and from school, and almost at once I saw him. Or, more accurately, smelled him, as he was leaning against a tree, smoking.

'Don't you ever stop? You'll kill yourself.' I knew I was nagging, but his doomed, romantic pose reminded me of our first meeting on the bridge, and I felt exasperated all over again. He was wearing the same old leather jacket, and his black hair fell over his brow in a dishevelled, poetic mop. By contrast, I felt all tarted up. I wished I hadn't worn mascara, or taken so much trouble with my hair. It looked as though I'd made an effort for his sake – which, of course, I had – when all the time he'd been lounging against his tree, certain that I was going to come.

'Yes, you're right.' Andy threw down his fag-end and stamped it out. 'But it is only hastening the inevitable end. Anyway' – he paused, looking me up and down – 'you certainly took your time.'

'I was waiting for Mum to leave,' I lied, aware that, besides looking all dolled-up and ridiculous, I was also going pink.

'So you didn't tell her you were coming here?'

'Of course not! I never tell my mother things if I can help it.'

'Neither do I.'

We grinned at one another cautiously, glad to find an excuse to stop bickering.

'Come on.' Andy held a branch aside for me with a courtly gesture and we walked on together to the crest of the hill.

'So if you don't tell your mother anything, why did you ask me to visit her?' I had just realized that I didn't know for certain if his mother was going to be at home. Perhaps I was going to an empty house, a large, scary, empty house, with a boy whom I hardly knew. My heartbeat, which had calmed down while I was sauntering, speeded up again.

'I thought she could tell you about the tarot.'

My beating heart plummeted. I'd been right. It wasn't me he cared about, but bringing me together with his fortune-telling mother.

'There you are. Le Château Byron. Drumglass House, actually.'

We had come out at the place where I had stood, only a fortnight ago, when I first saw the house. Yes, there it was, every bit as tumbledown in reality as it had become in my memory. Only one or two of the windows were curtained, including the one where I'd glimpsed the face.

'Last time I was here, I think I saw your mother at that window on the first floor.'

'Yes, that's her room. I thought you must've seen her

when you came racing out of the wood. It can be quite a shock to see signs of life in Drumglass.'

I didn't know what to say to that, so I compromised with: 'I hope she didn't see me and think I was trespassing.'

'Well, you are; we both are, strictly speaking. None of this land belongs to us any more.'

'Did it once?'

'It certainly did. The Byron domain, as far as the eye could see. But it was all sold off years ago.'

We'd continued along the path, and I was getting a better view of the house. I would've said it was exactly like Sleeping Beauty's castle, except that Dad is always banging on about avoiding clichés. Anyway, Andy and I soon reached the entrance, which was a sagging metalwork gate slung between two stone pillars, each of which was crowned with a heraldic animal. I felt that I should be saying something complimentary as we walked up the curving drive, but I was speechless. His home was, on the one hand, an actual castle – the turrets, the elegant stone steps which led up to the front door and the carved coat of arms over it – but it was also almost a ruin. If it hadn't been for a thread of smoke from one of the chimneys, I'd never have believed anyone lived there.

'Well?' Andy had come to a stop on the circle of gravel in front of the house, and despite his casual stance, hands in pockets, I felt that he was challenging me.

To gain time, I turned away and looked at the garden, a series of tufty lawns that sloped away into the advancing shrubbery. Beyond the wall I could see nothing but the high, bare hills, and I realized that I was, at last, in the elusive countryside.

'What an amazing view.'

'Yes. It is pretty good.'

I glanced at Andy and saw that his face had softened as he looked at the hills. So, despite his ironic attitude, I guessed that he was proud of his weird home.

'I think your house is wonderful.' And as Dad wasn't there to hear me, I added firmly, 'It's like something from a fairy story.'

Andy sniffed dismissively, and said, in his old tone, 'Oh, it's picturesque so long as you don't have to live in it, especially in winter. There's no heating at all except for the range and a couple of open fires.'

I knew I'd said the right thing. Obviously I had to admire the house so that he could continue to hide his real feelings about it.

'Is it very old?' I asked, as we crossed the gravel and climbed the steps.

'The bit with the turrets is, but most of the old house was knocked down in the seventeen-nineties when this bit in front was built. So it's comparatively modern.'

Modern! Our lovely old flat had only been Victorian, and as for our new house, the cement was barely dry!

Andy opened one leaf of the double doors and ushered me into the hall.

'Welcome to Drumglass House,' he said.

CHAPTER twelve

The house was just the same indoors as out: beautiful, but decayed beyond the point of mere scruffiness. An un-carpeted staircase curved upwards under a cracked skylight, and doors and panelling had been rubbed clean of paint in several places. Dry leaves remained unswept on the stone floor, and there was very little sense of having actually come inside, as the air in the stairwell was as cold as that on the hill and had the same autumnal smell of mushrooms and damp.

Luckily, Andy didn't wait for me to comment, but led me down a corridor which seemed to get darker and colder the further we progressed. Then he opened the last in a series of doors and we stepped into a large kitchen.

My first reactions were relief and surprise at finding myself in a room which was warm and smelled of coffee. I hadn't been expecting comfort of any sort in Andy's home. Then I looked around and realized that if I'd been forced to describe Drumglass as 'fairytale', this kitchen was like nothing so much as the cosy den of a family of furry, storybook animals. There was the old-fashioned range, the dresser with rows of blue-and-white plates, and the scrubbed table. The only false note was provided by the woman who looked up sharply at our entrance, so startled that her cup clattered down into its saucer, sending a small wave of coffee over the book she was reading.

It wasn't that she was odd in herself, but rather that she didn't fit into her surroundings. This kitchen called for a plump mother in an apron, whereas Andy's mother looked exactly like him.

I don't know why this should have surprised me, but it did. Perhaps because it meant that Andy was no longer unique. Like him, she had high cheekbones and narrow dark eyes. But what I really noticed was how nervous she seemed. After our entrance and her spectacular shudder, she went on staring at us as though we were a couple of wolves come padding into her safe little home.

'Christabel, this is Rosa McBride; she's come to live down the road,' said Andy, in an easy, casual tone, as though there was nothing in the least odd about his mother's behaviour.

'How do you do, Mrs Byron,' I murmured, following his lead.

As I spoke, Christabel began talking quickly and brightly. 'Rosa, how nice to meet you. Andy doesn't often bring his friends home, do you, Andy? There's coffee made, would you like a cup, but I can just as easily make tea, the kettle's on the boil.' She jumped to her feet, gesturing towards the range, where, sure enough, a big black witch's kettle simmered on the side of the hob.

However, I said, 'Coffee would be fine, thank you,' partly because it would be fine, but mostly because I didn't want to send her into a further tizz. I felt that making tea would simply be too much for her. And I also felt – no, I knew – that Andy hadn't told his mother that I was coming. My arrival had been a complete surprise.

Anyway, Andy said, 'Sit down, Christabel, I'll get more cups.'

I wondered if this was typical of their relationship, his mother flustering and Andy calming her down. Although I also realized, now that I saw them together, that it wasn't just in looks that they were similar. Andy didn't have Christabel's air of tension, but he did give the same impression of aristocratic disdain, as though real life was simply too much of a slog. He got through it by drifting around the woods, smoking, while all Christabel seemed to do was sit at home and drink coffee.

'Take your jacket off, Rosa, and come and sit down,' said Christabel in a more normal tone. She had re-seated herself obediently at the table, upon which stood a large cafetière, still more than half full, a jug of milk and, keeping the place on her opened book, a bowl of demerara sugar.

I sneaked a glance at her as I put my jacket on the back of a chair and sat down. Due to Mum's influence, I can't help but notice people's hair first and Christabel's, although pretty, being long and dark with just a few threads of grey, was definitely untended. Her fringe was shaggy, and the rest twisted carelessly into a knot. Her clothes were equally uncared for, a long, worn denim skirt and a pale green cardigan with a hole in the elbow. Over them, she wore a hessian pinny, with a roll of garden twine spilling out of the pocket, and looking at her hands, thin as Andy's, but dirty and callused, I realized that she'd probably just nipped in from the garden for a cuppa.

Yet despite everything, her old clothes, her lack of make-up or jewellery, she was beautiful. She had a classic loveliness quite different from Mum's arty, charity shop chic, and now, seeing the simplicity of Christabel's appearance, I wished all over again that I hadn't dolled myself up, and I really, *really* wished that I was wearing a snugly old jumper instead of the clingy black silk top. I'd worn it so seldom that I'd forgotten just how low the neckline was. Christabel would probably think I always dressed like this. I looked up and, sure enough, her gaze was resting on my bosom.

'Would you like a biscuit, Rosa?'

'Yes, please.' I took a chocolate biscuit from the tin that Andy had put on the table, being careful not to meet his eye. I only hoped that he wasn't staring at me as well.

'Coffee – I hope it's not too strong.' Christabel handed me a cup.

'What pretty china,' I said in a young-ladyish voice I didn't recognize as my own. But it *was* lovely. A fluted cup and saucer with tiny pink flowers rambling all over them. Very like my despised wallpaper, but somehow perfectly in place in Drumglass.

'My grandmother's wedding china – what's left of it,' said Christabel. 'I dare say it's silly to use it for every day, but it's so pretty, I can't bear to just keep it in the cupboard.' She spoke in the same social tone I'd been using, but with an accent even grander than Andy's. As she poured coffee for Andy and more for herself, I took a cautious sip of mine and discovered one reason for her being so on edge. It was the strongest I'd ever tasted. After one cup of this I could dance all night, and she seemed to drink it by the potful!

As I very carefully lowered the fragile cup to its saucer, Andy pushed the sugar bowl towards me. 'More sugar, Rosa? It is on the strong side.'

'I knew it would be too strong! That's how I make it when I'm by myself, don't you drink it if you don't like it, Rosa, I'll make another pot, or I can easily make you some tea, if you prefer.' Christabel looked almost ready to burst into tears, her long eyes wrinkling up at the corners.

'No, no, this is perfect,' I said, bravely taking another sip, followed by a big bite of my biscuit. They weren't the sort Mum buys, but sawdusty things, with a thin coating of fake chocolate.

'Rosa's interested in the tarot,' said Andy, diverting his mother's attention.

'You are?' Christabel, who'd been about to leap to her feet again, sank down, her lovely face alight with interest. 'I've been reading the tarot for years, since I was at college. It was all the rage then, but I've come to realize that it's a very serious subject. I think there's a tendency for people to trivialize it – not that I think you'd do that, Rosa.' For a moment she looked as embarrassed as I'd felt over the killer coffee and, feeling sorry for her, I began to understand where Andy's protective yet exasperated attitude came from.

'No, I'm serious,' I assured her. I wished that Andy wasn't there, because then I could've confided the extraordinary things that had happened the day before at Debs's. 'I found these cards when we moved house,' I continued, 'and I got interested.'

'Didn't you say you shouldn't use someone else's cards?' Andy spoke casually, but remembering how serious he'd been on the bus, I glanced over at him. He didn't look at me.

'Well, yes, that's the general rule.' Christabel laced her long fingers together and looked down at them seriously. 'Usually it's important not to let anyone else touch your cards – the vibrations, you know – unless you're reading for them. Do you know who these cards belonged to?'

She transferred her gaze to my face. Her eyes, unlike Andy's, had a green tinge to them. I tried to meet them with an innocent, little-girl look.

'I'm not really sure. Some old auntie, I suppose.'

'No one closer?'

There was something very slightly alarming in the way in which Christabel was looking at me.

'Oh no,' I said. This conversation was making me uncomfortable. If Andy's mum was even one tiny bit psychic she'd know by now that I was lying.

In fact, she did sound doubtful as she said, 'Well, I

suppose you could do some sort of ceremony – thank the previous owner, take them formally into your keeping; that sort of thing.'

'That's a really good idea,' I said. 'Thank you.' And it *did* seem a good idea. Perhaps it would kill off any bad luck which might be lurking around the pack.

'Of course,' Christabel continued, 'they might not be ready to belong to someone else.'

'It doesn't feel like that. It feels like they *want* to belong to me.' I'd spoken before I realized it, and I caught Andy looking at me. *What a nutter*, he must be thinking. Well, let him. What did his opinion matter beside his mother's? 'Ever since I found them, they seem to want me to use them,' I said firmly.

'They're probably bored with lying around,' said Christabel, perfectly seriously. 'How long do you think it is since anyone last read with them?'

I realized I had no idea. Perhaps not since before Mum and Dad got married.

'I don't know. Eighteen or twenty years, at least.'

'Twenty years?' When Christabel narrowed her eyes, they looked greener.

'It could be.' I was puzzled by her sudden intensity.

'Honestly, Christabel!' burst out Andy. 'You're talking even more rubbish than usual. How can an inanimate object get *bored*, for God's sake?'

Christabel, however, ignored him. 'And you're absolutely sure you've got no idea who these cards belong to?' she said again, speaking in an oddly conversational tone, as though she were asking me an ordinary question, yet was extremely interested in my answer.

'They could be anybody's,' I said.

Christabel's eyes were fixed on me. 'Do you have them with you?'

'Yes.'

'Let me see them.'

It would've been impossible to refuse. I reached behind me into my jacket pocket, took out the velvet bag, and placed it on the table between us. It lay there, soft and harmless as a kitten, yet Christabel actually fell back from it and her right hand flew to her breast, almost as though she were going to cross herself.

'Natasha!' she said. 'After all these years, Natasha Munro!'

CHAPTER thirteen

Andy and I both stared at her. I wanted to say something, but all the words I might've used had got jammed in my throat.

Then Andy said, 'Who the hell is Natasha Munro? Christabel? Rosa?'

He looked at our astonished faces. Christabel was staring from the bag to me with an expression I simply couldn't read.

'Natasha Munro,' repeated Christabel, making it sound every bit as silly a name as it actually is. 'This certainly is a surprise.' She gave a brief, hoarse laugh.

I looked wildly at Andy. How did his mother know Mum's name? She'd even recognized her bag – and found it every bit as alarming as Mum herself had done.

'Who is this Natasha? How did you know her?' said Andy, speaking very calmly and quietly.

'I certainly knew Natasha,' said Christabel, reverting to her bright, social manner. 'I never thought I'd see that bag of hers again – all that embroidery: it's quite a shock. Believe it or not, it was through her that I first became interested in the tarot. Is she some relation of yours, Rosa? I thought there was something familiar about you, but I couldn't put my finger on it.'

I avoided her question by asking one of my own: 'But when did you meet her?' I couldn't believe that there was a link between this eccentric, posh woman and my mother.

'We were at art college together. Twenty years ago.'

Mum had been to art college! I actually felt my mouth falling open and, although I knew how daft that looks, it was a full five seconds before I could snap it shut.

'Of course, she wasn't really part of my set,' Christabel was saying, still in her scarily merry voice. 'I didn't know her frightfully well, and then, of course, she left after the accident, if accident it was; but the worst one could say about Natasha was that she was a little bit of a— Well the kindest word would—'

'Christabel!' said Andy.

She went quiet, like a slapped child, but I was already on my feet.

'Don't you dare say anything about my – my family!' My voice was shaking, despite my attempt to keep it steady. 'You don't know anything about us. You just sit up here in this ruin of yours like – like a *spider*, so what could you know about *anything*?'

Christabel had opened her eyes very wide and was now watching me with a horrible air of satisfaction, as though I'd somehow fulfilled all her worst expectations. I just longed to take that look of disdain off her face.

'I always thought,' I said, 'that the mark of a good hostess was to make her guests feel at home.'

It actually worked. She made a tiny flinching movement, but simultaneously Andy got to his feet. I knew I'd gone too far, but I still took the final leap over the edge of polite behaviour.

'Nobody in *my* home would make rude remarks to a guest about their family,' I continued, picking up my jacket and clutching it, along with the velvet bag, to my quivering neckline. My heart was beating so hard that it almost seemed as though the tarot pack were throbbing alongside in sympathy. 'Please don't bother to show me out,' I said, addressing Andy, but without allowing myself to look at him. 'And thank you so much, Mrs Byron, for the *delicious* coffee.'

And with as much dignity as possible I swept from the room. Once in the flagstoned corridor I was afraid of getting lost, but retracing my steps I found myself back in the entrance hall. I rushed to the door and grasped the twisted metal handle. When it refused to turn I panicked, pulling and tugging, terrified of being trapped in what I now thought of as Christabel's lair.

'You have to push and turn at *precisely* the same time.'

I jumped, but the voice was Andy's. He opened the door and I found myself safely outside Drumglass, trembling, but glad to breathe the cold autumn air. I glanced uncertainly at Andy. Had I really just called his mother a *spider*, of all ridiculous things? Even the most yobbish lads at school wouldn't hear a word against their mums, so how would Andy ever forgive me?

And sure enough, although it was growing dark, I could see how coolly he was regarding me.

'You didn't need to speak to my mother like that,' he said in the same bitterly polite voice which she had used. 'She may seem a bit eccentric to someone like you from a *normal* family' – he made it seem the most tremendous insult – 'but that's no reason to be rude to her.'

His tone just made me angry all over again – yet the worst of it was that I couldn't say anything in my own defence without explaining that the cards were Mum's and that she was Natasha Munro. However, I certainly wouldn't let him know that I cared what he thought. Who were the Byrons to sneer at Mum and me?

'Excuse *me*,' I said. 'If it comes to insults, it was your mother who started it, and I'd sooner belong to a normal family than live in a dump like this.' I gestured grandly towards Andy's ancestral home. 'What's so special about you that qualifies you to despise me? You said it yourself, Andy Byron: you're not even related to the poet!'

And I turned and marched off down the gravel path without giving him a chance to reply. I didn't cool down until I was through the gateposts, crowned with their shadowy, cat-like beasts, and in the shelter of the wood. Then I stopped, breathless, under what I realized was the tree where Andy had waited for me. There was a single fag-end on the ground and I stepped on it hard, grinding it under the pine needles. It seemed hours since I had climbed the hill, my worst fear that I might show how flattered I was by Andy's invitation.

Pausing to put on my jacket, I was very aware of the empty, dark path along which Andy was not following me. And I didn't need to turn round to be aware of Drumglass, no longer a castle from a good fairytale; more like the Russian witch's tower, surrounded by a wall of skulls!

I set off down the field, sniffling a bit, rather than full-scale crying, but then, when I was halfway across, all the city lights snapped on at once and I stopped in astonishment, ankle-deep in damp grass. I'd never seen that happen before! Or I'd never been aware of it – not when I'd been down there in the actual streets. Now I was in the country, seeing things from a different angle.

Then, however, the lights reminded me of just how uncosy a hillside is, so I belted down the rest of the field, climbed the wall and only slowed down when I was level with the Parkers' front window. The last thing I wanted was to have anyone see me speeding home as though something dark and nameless were after me.

At my own gate I hesitated. I was still shivering but I wasn't quite ready to go indoors. How could I look Mum in the face now that I knew she had a secret? Having once been a student was perfectly normal – and yet she'd kept totally quiet about it! Then I remembered the scene in the kitchen a fortnight ago: Mum looking desolately at the shade cards, and Dad telling her it wasn't too late. Had he meant not too late to go back to art college?

And why had she left?

So instead of opening the gate, I went round the side of the garden until, from the shelter of the trees, I could see into the kitchen. And there was Mum, moving about with various painting utensils in her hands. I watched her, as Andy must've watched us. Perhaps, compared to his lonely life with Christabel, we really seemed to be a happy family.

And so we had been, although I hadn't appreciated it at the time. It was stealing the cards that had changed everything. I had a choice: I could go straight upstairs to Mum and Dad's room and put the cards back inside the chiffon dress; or I could find out their secret.

But it wasn't really a choice. In my pocket the old pack of tarot cards bumped against my thigh in a warm and comradely fashion. They knew I had already chosen.

I unlatched the back gate and went up the path, my trainers slapping on the stones, while Mum, oblivious, birled backwards and forwards in the light. When I opened the kitchen door she glanced round, yet didn't seem to notice that I looked as though I'd been pursued by Grannie's famous witches. I'd seen myself in the mirror and I had leaves in my hair and my eyes had gone absolutely huge in my white face.

'Rosa, there you are. I'm afraid it's just something frozen and salad again tonight. I've been that busy there was no time to cook. I've been tearing into Nairn's room, and when I'm done with that we'll do yours. I've brought some more shade cards so you can choose which purple you want.'

Mum waffled on, taking off her painting overall and rubbing her hands with a slice of lemon before she began making salad, while all I could do was stare at her. She'd been an art student and she'd never told me. She could read the tarot and she'd never told me. And she'd been involved in an accident which had ended her artistic career.

However, at any moment the real mother which the distant, fortune-telling Natasha had turned into was going to notice my odd behaviour, so I pulled myself together and said, 'Where's Dad?'

'Gone to pick up Nairn from his new wee friend Ed's. Isn't it wonderful he's made such a nice friend already?'

Not at all – only to be expected, I said to myself sourly. If I'd changed schools, I'd still be at the stage of desperately trying to fit in and wondering whether I should hang on until the cool people noticed me or whether I should settle for being pals with my fellow nerds.

But I'd *almost* had a new friend: Andy! That was such a painful thought that I focused on Mum instead.

There she was, still stotting about the kitchen, strands of red hair slithering free of their knot, and her face pink with effort and pleasure.

Without giving myself time to think, I opened my mouth and said, 'Mum, you're so good at all that interior dec stuff – didn't you ever think about going to art college?'

She stopped dead, a knife in one hand and a stick of celery in the other, like a vengeful priestess staying her hand while her victim gave a final squirm. Then, after only the tiniest pause, she resumed chopping and said, in an almost normal voice, 'Och no, hairdressing suits me just fine,' followed by, 'Those pears in the fruit bowl are too hard to eat raw; you peel them and put them on to simmer. We'll have them with ice cream and chocolate sauce.'

And without another word she went on slicing and mixing. I began on the pears – but I just couldn't keep quiet.

'I think it's a shame.' I said firmly, rather as Andy had spoken to *his* mother. 'You're loads better than all the arty people at school. And there's nothing to stop you going now. With Nairn at school all day you could cut back on your hairdressing, go to some classes and get a portfolio together. If you started now, you could probably be going to college in three years time.'

Mum stopped work again, her pink cheeks turning red. 'Rosa, what's got into you? I never heard such nonsense!'

'It's just such a *waste*!' I said passionately. I didn't quite know what had been wasted, or why, but I suddenly couldn't bear it. 'It's not just a waste, it's a *wicked* waste.'

'Well, Rosa, I had no idea that you held such strong opinions on how I choose to lead my life.' And Mum sounded so upset and offended that I realized the time had come to shut up.

'OK, sorry,' I said, but as she whirled away, clattering open a drawer, I just longed all the more to find out what had happened twenty years ago when, unbelievably, Mum and Christabel Byron had been students together.

CHAPTER fourteen

When I woke up on Sunday morning, I was actually relieved to find it was raining. In place of yesterday's sunshine, fronds of mist, much more in keeping with my dark mood, were drifting up the valley. I stood at the window in my T-shirt and pyjama bottoms, just steeped in misery from head to foot. The whole sinister and embarrassing scene with Christabel kept playing itself over in my head, followed by Andy's cool dismissal and Mum's anger.

If someone had told me a week ago that my own mother had a Dark Secret, I'd have laughed at them, but now I felt like moaning out loud. I could easily have done so – Tess of the D'Urbervilles would probably have made a plaintive little speech at this point – but it just seemed too dramatic. This was real life, *my* real life, not a Victorian novel or a TV soap, and as I'd got myself into this state of misery and confusion, it was up to me to get myself out.

I decided that there were two things that I could do. I'd make things up with Mum by offering to help with Nairn's room; and I'd speak to Dad. Dad, a great believer in rational thought, always says that problems are best solved logically rather than by intuitive muddling through, which is Mum's method. So the logical way of solving the art-college mystery would be to ask one of the other people who must know the truth: Dad.

Accordingly, I shuffled myself into my painting clothes and went downstairs, determined to get him on his own sometime during the morning.

I felt even worse, though, when Mum was pleased out of all proportion by my offer of help.

'Rosa, that's really sweet of you, but are you sure you haven't got homework? And you've already done your share of the living room,' she cried, looking up from her dainty breakfast of fresh fruit salad and yoghurt.

'It's no problem,' I said, slumping down beside Dad, who was tucking into a big bowl of porridge.

'The family who works together, lurks together,' he said, but as Nairn, presumably still asleep, wasn't there to laugh at his lurking impression, Mum and I groaned obediently.

Anyway, after breakfast we all got down to work, and it was coffee time before I had a chance to speak to Dad.

Seeing the rain thin down to drizzle, he'd rushed into the garden with his precious shelves, so, checking that Nairn and Mum were out of the way, I followed him.

Dad is actually hopeless at DIY, but he throws himself into it with wild enthusiasm. He had the wood all measured up and was sawing it into chunks, whistling a merry Scots reel as he worked.

I stood on the wet lawn, where yesterday's crunchy

leaves now lay like wet sweetie wrappers, and watched until he paused for breath.

'Dad, I was wondering . . .' I said, determined this time to approach the subject cautiously. 'Did Mum never think of going to art college? I suggested yesterday she got a portfolio together and she snapped my head off.'

I was watching Dad carefully while I said all this, so I saw the look of tremendous sadness that crossed his face before he reassembled himself into his serious teacher mode.

'Well, the thing is, Rosa,' he said, 'I think your mother feels she's missed the boat as far as higher education's concerned. She and I were very young when we married, and then you and Nairn came along, and she's always felt she couldn't afford to take time off to study. Believe me, I've tried to persuade her, but no one in her family has gone to college or university, and so she's no confidence in herself.'

While Dad was saying this, I felt colder and colder, as though the mist had turned into torrents of freezing rain. Dad was lying to me. Dad, who believed in the search for ultimate truth and stuff like that! I simply couldn't bear listening to him, so I muttered, 'Yeah, it's a pity, but I see what you mean,' and began sidling back towards the house.

I wasn't to escape so easily. Dad called me back.

'Now, I know it's frustrating, but it's best not to mention college to your mother. It only upsets her – as you've seen already.'

'OK,' I said. I'd also been planning to ask him some careful questions about Mum and the tarot, but now there didn't seem to be any point. I went into the house chilled and damp, and feeling that I'd been let down by some childhood superhero.

The rest of the morning passed in a miserable daze as I crawled around Nairn's floor painting the skirting board midnight blue, while Mum did some fancy stencilling. She was transforming the room into a magic cavern and, recovered from last night's huff, was singing along to a succession of folksters, from the Chieftains to Fergie Mac.

'You lilt at your needle,
You sing at your seam,
Bonnie red bird,
You stitch as you sing,' she warbled.

I didn't have the heart to insist on any of my music. Somehow my conversation with Dad hurt more than my having offended Andy, who wasn't, I reminded myself, actually a friend. Dad had always, *always* told me the truth. Whenever Mum might want to gloss over some awkward subject, Dad would treat it seriously. Until now.

Every so often I looked up at Mum, dabbing away with her stencil brush, or at Dad as he pounded up and down the stairs with bits of shelving, and my whole body ached with *ignorance*. My happy and devoted parents – and presumably Grannie as well – had a secret! All the ordinary old family life which I'd taken for granted was make-believe.

I pulled myself up. That wasn't really true. Compared to

loads of other families I knew, we *were* happy: Mum and Dad were together; we had enough money; and Nairn's asthma was the only thing to ruffle the smooth surface of our lives. But that was it! What lay *under* that surface?

If Mum and Dad wouldn't tell me, then probably Grannie wouldn't either. I could hardly go back to grim Drumglass and ask Christabel. And I'd already asked the tarot. I shuddered and took a huge sniff of paint fumes, as though I deserved to feel sick.

I'd just have to reconcile myself to not knowing. As Grannie was fond of saying: too much knowledge is a dangerous thing. Dad disagrees with this, arguing that it's a *little* knowledge that is dangerous, but he wasn't obeying his own advice.

So I went on painting, saying alternately to myself, Oh, Dad, oh, Andy Byron, until Mum had finished her prancing dragons and declared we could break for lunch.

When I'd finished my smoked cheese and mixed lettuce on rye piece, Mum almost pushed me out the door.

'Rosa, you're white as a sheet, it's thon oil paint. The rain's nearly stopped so you have a breath of fresh air before we do the next bit.'

So I put on my old boots and galumphed sorrowfully along the muddy road, thinking how it was only a fortnight since I'd had my first glimpse of Drumglass, a week since Andy and I had met in the moonlight, twenty-four hours since— All my black, guilty thoughts rose up inside me in a queasy, paint-drenched wave. Things had gone wrong from the very moment I'd skived off and seen Andy on the bridge.

I strode on and on, until I realized that without quite noticing I'd climbed the wall and was now halfway up the hill, and heading for Drumglass. I slowed down, taking big damp breaths. What on earth was I doing? I certainly wasn't up to knocking on the door, but if I should just happen to come across Andy, I could explain about Mum and the cards and perhaps he would understand and forgive me. I went on more hesitantly, but when I'd reached the trees and there was no familiar slouching figure and no smell of French ciggies, I circled right round Drumglass until I came to higher ground and could see over the wall and into the garden. And now I could see someone – Christabel – digging in the fine rain. She was turning over a vegetable patch, working so rhythmically that it was a pleasure to watch her. She was wearing a long skirt and a big heathery sweater and had a scarf tied over her head, so that she looked like some noble peasant woman, tilling the ancestral soil. I leaned against the drenched bark of a fir tree and watched as she performed mysterious garden tasks, going backwards and forwards with a wheelbarrow, exchanging a spade for a fork and then digging some more.

As I stood there, the rain thickened, but she worked on, and there was something in her distant, industrious figure that drained all the anger out of me.

So once upon a time she'd held some grudge against Mum, but now she was a lonely single parent, digging in the rain, while down the hill Mum was cosily painting Nairn's room to the sound of her beloved folk music, as Dad footered with his shelves. I actually began to feel sorry for Christabel – although not so sorry or so brave that I dared advance onto her property and apologize – so after a bit I turned round and went home. All the way down the hill I kept imagining that Andy would appear out of the wood or from behind our row of houses. But he didn't.

CHAPTER fifteen

When I went into school the next morning, the first person I met was Mrs Grier. Or rather, I didn't so much meet her, as was swept down upon by her.

'Rosa! What a wonderful, wonderful idea of yours to have a fortune-telling stall at the fair! It's bound to be a fantastic money-spinner – that type of thing's always tremendously popular.'

Mrs Grier is one of these young, energetic teachers, as yet unsquashed by school life, and now all that energy was being beamed at me like a deadly ray.

'I've spoken to Mrs Cuthbert and the art department will do you a nice booth, all signs of the zodiac, and you'll need a good big poster, won't you? Your friend Debs suggested "Gypsy Rosa, Seer to the Stars". That's very clever and snappy, I think, don't you?'

I was so appalled I literally couldn't speak. I just stood there like a stookie, while Mrs Grier, in her snazzy top and short, but not too short, skirt, yapped on at me until her glowing, lipsticked mouth seemed to take on a life of its own. 'It's always so good when pupils get involved, Rosa. I'm sure you'll find you get more out of the experience than you put in. I expect you can manage the costume yourself, can't you? I remember your mother made some wonderful costumes for the school play. Some of the money we raise this year's going to buy lighting equipment for the drama club and then we're also making a contribution to the children's hospice, so all the hard work's going to be for the best possible cause.'

The children's hospice! Now it would be impossible for me to refuse! Just wait until I saw Debs – I'd wring her neck: how dare she tell Mrs Grier that I'd be a gypsy without asking me first? And what if the strange power had deserted me and I couldn't do it? And, worst of all, Mum would find out I'd pinched her cards. So all the time I was apparently listening to Mrs Grier, part of my mind was racing in circles trying to remember whether Mum had said she *was* coming to the fair, or whether she'd said she *wasn't* because she had to take Nairn and Gavin to some fiddle competition. So, dredging up a last shred of common sense, I said, 'Actually, about the poster, I'd rather not be Gypsy Rosa, because then everybody would know it's me. Wouldn't it be more mysterious if I were – oh, Gypsy Zerlina?'

If Mum *did* come, she wouldn't realize that I was the exotic gypsy, and Debs could tell her I was busy with the teas or something. Of course, she was bound to find out eventually, but I'd deal with that when the time came.

'Good point, Rosa – whatever you think's best. You just

run along to Mrs Cuthbert at break and tell her what you want. I'll see you later.'

And off she went, clipboard in hand, ready to pounce on her next victim.

'I see you've been talking to Mrs Grier.' Debs had saved me the trouble of tracking her down by appearing at my side. 'She's really pleased that you've volunteered to appear at the fair.' My supposed friend was grinning complacently.

'But you know fine well I didn't volunteer!'

'You would've done once you'd thought about it. I just saved you the trouble.'

'But Debs, how *could* you?'

'Och, Rosie, you know you're longing to do it really. We'll make you this great costume. You'll be the star turn! And I'll get dressed up too and stand outside your tent and tell people how wonderful you are and organize the queue and take the money and everything.'

Now I saw it all. Debs was getting off on the idea of being the mystic's little helper. She really fancied the idea of herself in a gypsy costume with a low-cut bodice and a flashy tinselled scarf over her curls.

'Debs, you are a total *cow*,' I said. 'You know I can't do it. I don't know enough. It was OK at your house, but that was just you and Leanne and Marisa.'

'So what? You've got to admit you were absolutely spot on with them, and if you can't do it again at the fair, just do what you did with me and make it up.'

For the second time in five minutes, I was dumbfounded. Debs hadn't been taken in at all by her fake fortune! Because she acts so daft, I still forget, despite having known her all these years, how sharp she really is.

'Don't worry, I'm not going to tell anyone.' Then a smarmy, religious look came over her face. 'And it *is* for the children's hospice.'

'Oh, get to Falkirk!' I said, storming off. But I'd hardly stormed a couple of paces when I was surrounded by a group of kids from my class.

'Is it true you're going to tell fortunes at the fair, Rosa?'

'Can you really tell fortunes?'

'She can not – it'll be a huge scam.'

'Will you do mine?'

'It'll be bari to have fortune-telling.'

'Do you use a crystal?'

Now I knew what it felt like to be a reluctant star mobbed by the press. And to make it worse, over the girls' tossing bunches and tails, and the boys' bristles and quiffs, I could see Clary making her disdainful way into the classroom. She'd obviously heard about my psychic exploits and now she'd never speak to me again.

My prediction about Clary soon came true. She managed to avoid me at break, and at lunchtime she disappeared into the music room with her flute and a bunch of droopy fellow instrumentalists. As I watched her go, I realized how much time I'd been spending with her lately, especially since Debs had begun hanging out with Franklin. It was Clary with whom I always ate my deli sandwiches now, as we discussed films and TV programmes and the books we'd been reading. I'd even thought of telling her about Andy. And I was desperate to apologize to her for lying about my visit to Debs.

It just seemed that ever since stealing the cards I'd got more and more tangled up in all the lies I was telling *and* all the things I was hiding. I'd always thought that as I got older I'd become more sensible and maybe even nicer, like Nairn, but it didn't seem to be happening.

One thing, however, was clear. I'd lost Andy's friendship before I'd even gained it, so I simply couldn't lose Clary's as well. Accordingly, when school was over, I waited for her in the playground. Whether or not she was hiding from me, she certainly took her time, and when she eventually emerged, still escorted by a couple of orchestra friends, I was hopping up and down with cold. The weather had changed overnight, tilting towards winter.

'Hi, Clary,' I said, advancing bravely. 'Can I speak to you?'

The two friends, who'd been laughing at some wildly funny rehearsal joke about a brass player who didn't diminuendo along with everyone else, looked at me scornfully, as did Clary herself.

'I want to explain about Friday,' I said.

One of the friends, a girl who wears her hair in perky bunches to disguise the fact she's in the orchestra, said loudly, 'Come on, Clary, if we go back to my house we'll have time to run through the adagio,' while the other closed in like a loyal collie dog protecting a lamb from a wolf.

In the face of all this musical support, I despaired. Clary

would be swept away from me on a tide of Italian. I turned away, only to hear her saying, 'It's OK, we can practise tomorrow. I'll chum you to your bus stop, Rosa.'

We waited until the friends had said a surprised goodnight and turned away down the street.

'I'm really, really sorry,' I said. 'I know I should've told you why I was going to Debs's, but you'd said all that stuff about reading the tarot being the first step on a downward path, so I knew you'd disapprove.'

'But why did you read the cards for these tattie-heads in the first place?' Clary went through the school gates and I followed her. As well as all her usual books, she was carrying her flute case and a folder of music.

'They wanted me to,' I faltered. It was even more difficult than I'd expected to tell the truth. 'What happened was, I did it because it was exciting and it made me feel important. So there you go.' And I glared straight ahead, daring her to despise me.

'All right then, but that was in private: you didn't have to go and say you'd do it at the fair.'

'I didn't!' I exclaimed. By this time we were walking side by side towards the main road, but I stopped for a moment and waved my arms for emphasis. 'Debs arranged the whole thing behind my back. When I came in this morning, Mrs Grier leaped on me and told me it was all set up.'

'And you just went along with it?'

'What else could I do? It's not just for the school, it's for the hospice – it would've looked awful if I'd backed down.'

'Yes, I see.'

As Clary was finally sounding more sympathetic, I continued, 'And Mum's going to *skin* me when she finds out. She really hates fortune-telling, just like you.'

'But I thought you said you'd found those cards at home?'

It was as hard to fox Clary as it was Debs.

'They were in a box of old junk,' I said. 'I found them when we were flitting. I suppose they might've been Mum's originally, but she certainly doesn't agree with any of that stuff now.'

That was as near the truth as I dared go and I prayed Clary would accept it. Luckily all she said was, 'Well you *have* got yourself into a mess, haven't you?'

'Yes,' I said humbly. 'You were dead right, Clary, it *is* a downward path. I just took one little step and it's got worse and worse.'

Quite how much worse I couldn't tell even Clary.

Clary, however, was laughing outright, something she rarely does. 'Oh, Rosa, I didn't mean it *literally*!'

'But that's how it's turned out,' I said miserably, as we reached my bus stop and I joined the queue of equally gloomy fellow commuters.

'Do you have to go straight home? We could go for a coffee.'

This was such a major peace offering that I hated to refuse. 'I'd love to, but if I'm late Mum worries about me going up the road in the dark.'

'Tell you what, your house is at Burnshead, isn't it? My

mother teaches at the new media department on Mondays, and that's just down the road. If I come back with you, she could pick me up.' Clary shifted her books and conjured her mobile into her free hand. 'Would your mother mind?'

'Of course not.' Clary was being so much nicer than I deserved that I felt a small slice of my gloom detach itself and eddy up into the fluorescent twilight. 'Look, I'll call her and you call yours.'

Five minutes later, having fixed things with our respective mothers, we were aboard the bus and sitting on the big back seat, just like proper giggly teenagers – except, of course, that neither of us were giggling: Clary because she doesn't do that sort of thing, and me because I still had too much on my mind. I was also wondering how many of my problems I could share with Clary now that she'd decided to forgive me. Mum's secret seemed too private, while I was afraid that Clary would just be sarcastic if I tried to tell her about Andy. She thinks that boys are too childish to be taken seriously.

However, as we approached Andy's stop, I grew more and more twitchy, and simply couldn't concentrate on Clary's explanation of the rehearsal joke. Would he get on this bus, which was the later one? And if he did, would he think I'd hung around especially to see him? This was such a horrible thought that I slithered down in my seat, glad that I was in the far corner and practically hidden by Clary's huge mound of possessions.

'Honestly, if we're going to have that piece ready for our performance at the fair, people have to take their practising more seriously. I mean, it's not really funny to play loudly on purpose when everybody else is quiet.'

I was nodding along with this, pretending to listen, when my body simultaneously tensed, froze and prickled all over.

Andy had boarded the bus. I peered cautiously round Clary. Would he pretend not to see me and go upstairs, or would he really not see me and go upstairs anyway? This was an even worse prospect than having him think I'd been waiting for him, so I undid my slither by inching up a little. I couldn't do anything too obvious, because Clary would be disgusted if she saw me trying to catch the attention of a mere boy.

Andy, however, had already seen us, and was making his way down the aisle.

'Hi, Rosa,' he said, swinging his bag down off his blazered shoulder. He wasn't smiling. 'OK if I sit here?'

As there was loads of room next to Clary, this was probably part of his famed private school manners, so I said, 'Of course, fine,' and then, when Clary looked enquiringly from one of us to the other, I made a huge effort and said, in as normal a voice as possible, 'Clary, this is Andy; he lives near us.'

Although I'd tried to sound ordinary, to my horror my voice came out all posh, like Christabel's, so that I was afraid Andy might think I was imitating her.

However, he barely looked at me, but settled himself on the seat while Clary moved some of her stuff.

'Hello, Clary,' he said. 'Is that a flute case?'

'Yes, it is. Do you play an instrument?' she said eagerly, scenting another enthusiast.

'No, but my friend Ben's sister does. That's how I recognized the case.'

'That's not Ben Ramsay, is it? Ben and Stephanie. He goes to your school.'

'Do you know old Benjie? We're on the magazine committee together.'

'I haven't seen him for years. We used to be neighbours, and he and Stephanie and I played together when we were kids, but then they moved house and went to different schools, so we lost touch.'

And Clary and Andy were soon chatting away about the amazing coincidence and exchanging anecdotes about this Ben and his talented sister and finding other people whom they both knew and saying how odd it was that they'd never met when they had so many pals in common.

While this was happening, I sat in my corner, alternately glad that I wasn't having to join in and resentful because I was being left out. I watched Clary, thinking that if I hadn't known her so well, I'd almost have said that she was flirting. She wasn't doing any of the obvious Debs-type stuff like trilling with girlish laughter or unbuttoning her jacket, but she'd gone a very light pink and at one point she actually tossed her pigtail back over her shoulder. Andy, meanwhile, totally ignored me, and I was soon reduced to staring out of the window, feeling like the plain best friend in a high-school movie.

But a shiver went through me when, through my cross

dwam, I heard Andy say, 'And do you read the tarot, like Rosa?'

'Certainly not!' exclaimed Clary, predictably. 'In fact, I've been warning her against it.'

'Really?' said Andy, with what I felt was a nasty degree of relish.

'But she wouldn't listen to me, and it serves her right, because now she's been roped in to read fortunes at our autumn fair on Saturday.'

I was actually quite glad to hear Clary say this because, first of all, it meant I wouldn't have to confess this to Andy myself, and secondly, it showed that even Clary could behave in a sneaky, vengeful way if she felt like it.

'Really?' said Andy again, but this time addressing me. 'But can you actually do it? Tell fortunes?'

'I can too,' I said, defending my new-found professional skill. 'I told some girls' fortunes last week and I was totally right. I even told one girl she was going to be a bridesmaid and no one else knew about it, not even her best friend.'

'But that must've been a coincidence,' said Andy. 'Every girl's a bridesmaid at some time or another, aren't they, Clary? Stephanie's been one about five times.'

I hated this Stephanie. Had Andy been to any of the weddings and seen her in her simple gown with a coronet of fresh spring flowers on her undoubtedly blonde hair?

'You're right,' said Clary. 'I've been one twice and my sister's been a flower girl.'

Now I hated Clary as well.

'Coincidence or not,' I said, glaring at my so-called

friend, 'I've got to do it. It *is* for the children's hospice. *And*,' I added for Andy's benefit, 'I'm going to have the most beautiful gypsy costume.'

At this, both Andy and Clary burst out laughing in the exaggerated way in which younger, sillier people behave on buses, and then, before I could say anything else, dignified or otherwise, Andy got to his feet.

'My stop.'

We were drawing up at the little mall, and I felt a pang as I remembered his basket of dreary fodder.

Andy, of course, not having read my mind – as he sometimes used to do, I sorrowfully reminded myself – was still chuckling.

'Nice to have met you, Clary. I'll remember you to Ben and Steph.'

'Yes, give them my love. Tell Stephanie to give me a call. Wait – I'll give you my number.' And Clary, who is mega-organized despite her dreamy appearance, produced a card with her name and mobile number, and handed it to him.

Andy nodded and put it in his pocket. 'OK, Clary. Bye, Romany Rosa.' And away he went, down the aisle, off the bus, and in a moment had disappeared into the bright cube of the shopping centre.

'Well!' said Clary, falling back into her seat. 'You never told me about *him*.'

'There's nothing to tell,' I said, trying not to sound sulky. 'I just see him on the bus sometimes.'

I hoped I wasn't blushing as I told yet another lie, but if I were, Clary apparently didn't notice as she went on about the famous Ben and Stephanie and what a surprise it had been meeting Andy.

When she finally ran down I said, 'Remember, not a word to Mum about the fair.'

'But the first thing she'll see when she comes in the door is your gypsy caravan or whatever.'

'No, there's a good chance she's ferrying Nairn to some fiddle thing. And if she does come, she won't know I'm Gypsy Zerlina until, well, until . . .'

For the third time that afternoon, Clary began to laugh, and I reflected sourly that at least I was giving her a lot of amusement.

'This is where we get off,' I snapped, as the bus headed out into bungalowville. 'Shall I take that bag for you?'

'Oh right, thanks, Rosa. I see what you mean, we are in the middle of nowhere, aren't we?' And Clary followed me off the bus, still chatting gaily.

In fact, I'd seldom heard her talk so much. As we set off up the hill together – it was now cold as well as dark – I realized that she almost sounded like Debs. And not Debs in general, but Debs when she went on about Franklin.

It was not only Mum who had a secret side.

CHAPTER sixteen

The next couple of days dragged past so slowly that I might've been wading through platefuls of Grannie's famously stodgy lentil soup. Get up in the morning, trail to school in the autumn drizzle, make myself chat un-suspiciously to Clary, assure Debs that I was practising the spreads, travel back home on a doleful, Andyless bus, and then wonder, while I watched Mum serving supper, if I hadn't just *imagined* the entire scene with Christabel.

The only bit of good luck was that Mum couldn't come to the fair as it was her turn to take Nairn and Gavin to their music festival. I realized, of course, that one of her old friends was bound to tell her about my unexpected performance, but at the moment I didn't have the energy to worry about it.

Thursday was exactly the same as Tuesday and Wednesday, and by the end of school I felt so dismal that I hung about until I'd missed the early bus and took the later one. I had to speak to Andy. If only Clary hadn't been with me on Monday – but if I'd been alone perhaps he would've ignored me entirely. Perhaps he only joined us because of her creamy skin and shiny toffee hair.

However, I wasn't to find out because there was no sign of him. Was he avoiding me? Or even worse, was he, at this very minute, meeting Clary, who'd raced away with some feeble excuse the moment the bell had rung? If I hadn't been fenced in by newspaper readers and tired women with their cross kids, I would've cried for sheer misery. As it was, I actually began to sniff, and had to take deep breaths of the germ-laden air until I had control of myself.

Then I pulled out my tarot book. It was one thing to read the cards for Debs and the girls, but quite another to do it for strangers – strangers who would actually be crossing my palm with silver. Looking at the book, however, just made me feel worse. Every page I turned revealed hearts cruelly stabbed, or doomed voyagers setting out across a dark lake.

What would I do if one of my clients turned up these terrifying cards? I wished I'd been able to explain to Clary just how miserable I felt about the fair, but first of all she'd laughed, and now, since our meeting with Andy, she'd gone a bit peculiar. She wasn't actually avoiding me, but she spent a lot of time checking her mobile – a very unClary-like activity – and both yesterday and today she'd absolutely scuttled out of school instead of doing her usual elegant, book-laden drift.

She didn't fancy Andy, did she? Well, why not, when I did? Not that I actually fancied him in *that* way, I told myself sternly. This was actually worse. He'd seemed like a friend. He'd understood how I felt when Mum and Dad put

Nairn first. He'd invited me home to meet his mother – and just look how I'd behaved! Well-brought-up Clary would never be rude to a parent, no matter how insulted she felt. *And* she was serious and clever, far more Andy's type than I was.

Luckily we were approaching my stop, so before I could embark on a full-scale fantasy of having to sit behind Andy and Clary on the bus while they held hands and discussed the day's *Guardian*, I stuffed the tarot book into my bag and struggled down the aisle.

Once I'd jumped off the bus and seen its lights disappear, I turned up the hill. There wasn't any point in obeying Mum's instructions to call her for a lift if I were late, because this was her day for senior citizens' specials at a sheltered-housing complex, after which she'd go to pick up Nairn from orchestra. But I didn't care how dark it was. Lost in my own gloom I trudged upwards, and when I reached the short cut, I didn't think twice about turning off the road and into the woods.

It was much, much darker, but I pushed aside the brambles, pretending that I wasn't going this way because it just happened to be Andy Byron's route home. I wondered if he still stopped to look in at our window, or whether he now marched disdainfully past. I was climbing the last few metres, telling myself that I was out of breath, not sniffling, when I stopped short, suddenly truly breathless. Just ahead of me I could see a tiny red light, rising, pausing and falling.

'Hey, Rosa,' said Andy, dropping his cigarette and

stamping it out. 'You got the wrong bus. It really is too cold to hang about waiting for you.'

'What do you mean, *I* got the wrong bus?' I said, clinging onto every shred of dignity I'd ever possessed. This was difficult, because my previously heavy heart was now bounding and skipping in what I could only describe as my bosom. Andy was actually waiting for me, and he must've been there for at least half an hour! He wasn't in a café somewhere with Clary; he was waiting for *me* in the cold.

'*You* got the wrong bus,' I continued, as coolly as possible. 'I was on yours.'

I wondered if it would be OK to laugh, or whether I should just stand there, knee-deep in briars, enjoying this amazing feeling of being both flattered and happy. Except that the second I allowed myself to be happy, I began to wonder just why he was waiting. Probably he just wanted to tell me off for slagging his mum.

I took a huge deep breath. 'Look, Andy,' I said, 'I'm really sorry I was so rude to your mother. I would've told you on Monday but Clary was there.'

'Oh, the chaperone,' said Andy mockingly.

'I didn't know she was coming until the last minute,' I said, exasperation piercing through my pleasure, rather as the brambles were prickling through my jeans. 'In fact, she suggested it, not me. This wasn't some girly "you chum me so's I don't have to speak to him" thing.'

I was doing it again. Half a minute's conversation with Andy Byron and all my plans to be cool and sophisticated were in tatters.

However, he actually laughed. 'No, I didn't think I was that important. It was just, I was all ready to tell you that *I* was sorry and there you were with your friend.'

I listened carefully, but he didn't seem to be putting any special meaning into that final word.

'The thing is,' he continued, 'I *am* sorry. For what Christabel said. She doesn't see many people, cooped up in Drumglass, so she forgets how to behave in company. She should've realized this Natasha might be some relation of yours.'

She realized fine well, I thought, but what I said was, 'It's fine, I understand.'

'No, you don't,' said Andy. 'You don't understand about Christabel. No one does. That's why I don't usually take people home.'

My heart, which had been beating more calmly, leaped up again. He didn't take people home but he'd taken me!

'What's there not to understand?' I said, adding cautiously, 'I mean, she's a bit, well, nervous, but everybody's parents are peculiar in one way or another.'

Simultaneously we both glanced towards my dark house.

'So where are your peculiar parents? It's usually all go in the McBride household.'

'You can't have been watching us very carefully,' I said, 'or you'd know everyone's late on Thursdays. Come on, let's go inside, it's freezing.'

'I thought you'd never ask,' said Andy, following me through the gate. 'I've been waiting under that tree for so long that squirrels were hiding acorns in my pockets.'

I unlocked the back door and switched on the light, trying to look as though I were always bringing boys back home.

'Sit down,' I said, waving him towards the kitchen table while I put on the kettle and pulled the curtains. 'Tea, coffee?' Mum hadn't painted her way round to the kitchen yet, so it was still a feeble primrose with grey worktops. Compared to Andy's Beatrix Potter kitchen it looked painfully ordinary but fortunately, like most boys, he wasn't taking any interest in his surroundings. Instead, he was looking at me, which was a lot worse. I took off my coat, very aware that all I was revealing was my old jeans and a fleecy T-shirt. It would almost have been better to be wearing my tight black top.

'Whatever,' he said.

'Sorry?' I jumped.

'Tea, coffee, *whatever*.'

'Oh, uh, right. I'll make some coffee then; it won't be as strong as your mother's, though.'

'And a good thing too. Christabel's bad enough without being a caffeine junkie.'

'But is she always so, well . . .' I didn't quite know how to put it, but Andy smiled apologetically.

'Yes, but not to that extent.'

I remembered the huge leap she'd given when I'd appeared in the kitchen doorway.

'Hadn't you told her I was coming?'

'Was it that obvious?'

'Well, yes, it was.'

'The thing is, if I'd told her that someone was dropping in she'd probably have hidden in her room or the garden all afternoon.' Andy said this while looking straight ahead at Mum's Treasures of the National Gallery calendar.

'Hide from me!' I exclaimed, although, even as I spoke, I could believe him. It was easy to imagine the startled woman making for the stairs in great bounds like a fleeing gazelle.

'That's how neurotic she is,' said Andy. He sounded either bored or resigned and I stared at his profile, trying to make out what he was feeling. 'Like I said, she doesn't see many people. Doesn't go out much.'

'But why?' I put the cafetière down on the table and turned away to fetch a couple of mugs. Like Christabel, we actually possess dainty old china, but I didn't reckon on Andy's appreciating it.

'She likes being at home. She does a lot of gardening and she embroiders and makes rag rugs and stuff for a gallery which a friend of hers owns.'

'But doesn't she at least go to the shops?' I'd thought that perhaps Andy did the shopping because his mother was ill, but if she could work in the garden, there was no reason why she couldn't walk down the hill to the supermarket.

'She's scared,' he said in a low voice. He didn't look at me but concentrated on stirring sugar into his coffee.

'Scared? Scared of what?'

'This, that, the other.' He paused, and then said, 'Going out mostly. Agoraphobia, it's called.'

'I've read about it, I do know what it's called,' I said indignantly, but my indignation was to cover my surprise as several things thunked into place. Now I could begin to understand Andy and Christabel's weird lifestyle.

'Sorry, sorry. At least you can call it by its name, but she won't.'

'What do you mean?'

'If she gave it a name, she'd be admitting she was ill. As it is, she pretends that she could walk out of the gate any time she wanted. And as long as I'm here, that's exactly what she can do. Pretend.'

Andy's voice was as bitter as Christabel's coffee. When he still didn't look at me, I sat down beside him and touched his arm. For a second my grubby, biro-stained paw lay on his sleeve. 'I'm sorry,' I said. 'How long has she been – I mean, since . . . ?'

'Only really bad for the last couple of years. You know, when you're young, whatever your own family does seems normal, no matter how odd it might seem to other people. Then, after Dad left, she just got worse and worse.'

'But isn't she getting treatment?'

Andy's whole face narrowed, closed in on itself. 'She's too scared to actually *go* to the doctor's, that's the whole problem. I went to him myself last year and explained the situation, and he said he could refer her to a psychiatrist if she wanted help. But the thing is, she doesn't want it.'

Andy stopped, so I said, 'Doesn't want help? But couldn't the doctor do anything?'

Andy sighed in an exasperated sort of way. 'I should've

known it wouldn't work out. He came round to see her and she put on her "lady of the manor" act, wouldn't admit there was a thing wrong with her, and the doctor went away believing she was simply one of these scatty aristocrats who prefer staying at home and messing about in the garden.'

'So it didn't do any good?'

'Absolutely none. In fact, it made things worse. Christabel was so furious she hardly spoke to me for a week. Quite an achievement considering she's got no one else.'

'But you were only trying to help!'

'Not to her way of thinking.'

'But doesn't she want to get better?'

'She doesn't want things to change.'

It made a screwy sort of sense. 'I dare say it's too scary.'

'Yes, she'd have to do all these grown-up things like earning a living.'

I stared at him. 'But you've got money, haven't you?'

Andy laughed, but not cheerfully. 'What gave you that idea?'

'Well, your school, and the house—'

'God, that school! I'm only there because my grandfather left money in a trust for my education, and that's the school he and Dad both went to. The house is the family place, but Dad's new wife wouldn't live in Drumglass if you paid her.'

'Couldn't you sell it then?'

'Drumglass isn't the sort of place you *sell*.'

I'd obviously said the wrong thing, because Andy was looking at me with familiar disdain. 'Anyway, it'll be mine someday.'

'Yours!' My voice came out in a sort of horrified squeak.

'Yes. Eldest son and all that. Would it really be so bad?'

For the first time he looked around the kitchen and I could see him taking in the scuffed Formica and vinyl-tiled floor.

'No, no, of course not,' I said humbly. 'I'm sorry.'

To my surprise, Andy grinned. 'Don't be. You're absolutely right.' He took another sip of his coffee. 'Mmm, better than Christabel's. Anyway, I'm sorry she was so awful. Is this Natasha your aunt? You said the cards had belonged to an auntie.'

I took a deep breath. 'No. She's not an aunt. Tasha's my mum. Munro's her maiden name.'

I looked down at my hands, which were twisting together in my lap, so that I wouldn't have to see his reaction.

'Your mother? Jesus, Rosa, why didn't you say?'

'I'm sorry,' I said again. 'I should've told you. These cards were Mum's, she'd even embroidered her name on the bag that your mother recognized, but when I found them, she went – she was very upset.'

'Like Christabel,' said Andy.

We looked at one another and, although the heating had long since clicked obediently on, I felt cold.

'So your mother didn't recognize me then? I thought she might've said something after . . . after . . .'

'Not a word. But she does that. Goes silent. Especially after anything's, well—'

'Cake,' I said, jumping up. 'I forgot to offer you some cake.'

Mum loves baking, and although she doesn't eat much of her own work in the interests of her slender figure, she keeps the tins full for Nairn and Dad and me.

'Here you go.' I placed one of Mum's chocolate layer specials on the table. 'Can I interest you in a slice of pure carbohydrate?'

'Can't you just?' Andy was staring at the cake with an almost embarrassing amount of longing, and remembering his frugal shopping basket, I realized that the food that I took for granted might be a total luxury to him. So I cut him a huge slice, and a smaller one for myself.

'Amazing.'

Andy had taken a bite almost before I'd sat down again, and now looked the nearest to happy I'd ever seen him. It was enough to make me want to learn to bake, but that would really be a super-girly thing to do. Clary wouldn't stoop to making a boy his favourite nosh. Or would she?

'So our mothers actually knew one another?' Andy had wolfed half his slice, and had now slowed down enough to speak.

'I know. I can't believe it.'

'It's not really so odd when you think about it. They must be about the same age, so they'd have gone to art college at the same time—'

'But Mum never told me that she'd been to art college!'

'You mean she was an art student once and she kept it a

secret? But that's ridiculous! It's hardly something to be ashamed of.'

'But you heard what your mother said: *my* mother left after this mysterious accident.'

Our eyes met, and we were both silent for a long minute.

'And they don't seem to have exactly been best friends,' he said eventually.

'Understatement.'

'So what does your mother say about her past?'

'Oh, left school, went to work in a hairdresser's, did a course at tech, became a stylist, met Dad.' I thought for a bit. 'Actually, she doesn't speak very much about being young. Not after she left school or before she met Dad.'

'You mean there's a gap?'

I nodded. 'I've never noticed it before, but yeah. And I do know her first job after school was in Glasgow. She went to stay with her cousins, but I never thought that was strange. I mean, everyone wants to leave home.'

'True,' said Andy.

I looked at him, but when he didn't elaborate, I continued, 'What about Christabel, does she talk about college?'

'All the time. Her golden age, belle of the ball – by her account, that is – before she had the misfortune to marry Dad and get herself marooned at Drumglass.'

'So for some reason *my* mother left college after this accident while *your* mother was leader of the pack?'

'Looks like it.'

I couldn't express my confused feelings while sitting staring at the remains of the cake – Andy had demolished a second chunk – so I jumped up and paced round the table.

'It's the cards, Andy,' I said. 'It has to be the cards.' The Death card, I almost said. I put my hand to my mouth, and sat down again. 'Both our mothers went mental when they saw them again. Something happened connected to the cards. Something . . . something bad.'

'Or worse than just bad.'

My raised hand fell back into my lap. 'Oh, Andy,' I whispered. 'I asked the tarot. And I drew the Death card.'

'And I suppose you believe that has some deep significance?'

'Yes – yes, I do.' Hadn't I been worrying about that wretched card ever since I'd drawn it?

'Oh, Rosa, it's just another coincidence. The cards don't *mean* anything.'

'You said yourself something terrible must've happened.'

'But I was speaking logically.' Honestly, he was just as bad as Dad. 'Whatever happened had a serious effect on both our mothers, therefore . . .'

But I'd stopped listening. The garage door had slammed shut.

CHAPTER seventeen

I jumped to my feet. 'Would you like some more coffee?' I said loudly and politely. 'Another slice of cake?'

Andy had heard the noise as well. 'It was absolutely delicious, but no more, thank you.'

'So glad you enjoyed it,' I said, as the door opened and Nairn bounded in. He stopped short at the sight of my visitor, so surprised that he simultaneously dropped his rucksack and clutched his violin.

'Oh, hi, Nairn,' I said, hoping that Andy wouldn't realize, from my little brother's wide eyes and open mouth, that I didn't usually entertain boys in the family kitchen – or anywhere else, for that matter. 'This is Andy. He lives further up the hill. We come back on the bus together.'

I raised my voice for the benefit of Mum, who had appeared in the doorway behind Nairn. For a second she looked as amazed as Nairn, but stepping forwards into the light, she gave a big, stagy smile, and I could tell she was delighted to see me with a male visitor. Her wee girl growing up at last; happy hours ahead during which I finally allowed her to do my hair and buy me clothes – ending up with a spectacular wedding dress. And then her smile faded, to be replaced by a slight frown. Of course: Andy looked so like Christabel!

Andy had got to his feet and was holding out his hand, every inch the private schoolboy. 'How do you do, Mrs McBride? Rosa gave me a slice of your fantastic cake.'

Mum, mesmerized, shook his hand, while Nairn, the wee rat, continued to stare as though an alien had beamed down into our midst.

'Time I was off,' said Andy, shouldering his bag. 'Thanks for the coffee, Rosa. It was nice to meet you, Mrs McBride.'

'Go out the front way, it's quicker,' I said, ushering him past my still dumbfounded family and into the hall. I shut the kitchen door in Nairn's face and hurried Andy down the hall and out into the porch.

'So that's the famous little brother?'

'In person.'

'And your mother.'

'Yes.' Seeing Mum so cheery and, well, normal, it was harder than ever to imagine her as either a fellow student of Christabel's or as the participant in a supernatural crime.

'I don't think Mum recognized you,' I said. 'I thought she might have – I mean, you look so like—'

'She'd hardly be expecting a relative of her old . . . adversary – whatever.'

'We've got to find out what happened.' I stamped up and down on the cold floor.

'Do we really need to know?' Andy had gone down the

two concrete steps, and we looked at one another over the railing. We were now the same height. 'I get the impression our mothers don't want to be reminded of the past.'

'But the truth shouldn't hurt.'

'If you really thought that, Rosa, you'd have asked your mother by now.' And he set off down the path, leaving me alone under the porch roof. He was right, of course. I could easily have asked Mum if she'd ever met a woman called Christabel – but I hadn't.

Andy stopped at the gate. 'See you on the bus tomorrow?'

I managed to sound only mildly disappointed as I said, 'No, we've all got to stay on to set things up for the fair.' What I really wanted to do was give huge wolf howls. Andy offered to meet me and I couldn't because of that wretched fair!

I wondered if he might suggest doing something on Sunday, but he just said, 'Then I dare say I'll run into you sometime next week. Night, Rosa.' He opened the gate and then paused, making my whole pathetic body give a hopeful quiver. 'Good luck on Saturday, and remember me to your friend.' And off he went, loping along the dark road.

Lights were coming on the length of Burnshead, cosy orange or cool television-blue, in houses that looked tiny against the bulk of Andy's hill. I stamped again. If Andy Byron thought I was going to spend all next week wondering which bus to catch, just for the pleasure of his company, he had another think coming.

Always provided I actually survived until next week. The dreadful image of myself in a gypsy dress, which I'd managed to suppress while I was watching Andy eat cake, rose up again. Myself tongue-tied, muddling the cards—

'Has your boyfriend gone then?' Nairn burst out of the kitchen.

'He is *not* my boyfriend,' I said, shutting the door on the night. Remember him to Clary? I pushed past Nairn, who refrained from yelping when I stood on his toe.

'Well,' said Mum, unpacking her shopping at the table. 'What a very well-spoken young man.'

Had she recognized Andy? I sneaked a look at her. She was wearing her hair down, and it hung to her shoulders in fairytale curls. She tugged at a lock, frowning. 'Where did you say he lived, Rosa?'

'Just beyond the next stop.'

'He can't live in a wee house like this.'

I sighed with a mixture of relief and annoyance. Mum wasn't puzzled because Andy looked familiar, but because, to her way of thinking, he was a toff. Despite running her own business, and despite years of being friends with people like Gavin's parents, Mum still sees herself as the hairdresser's apprentice from Gorgie.

'There's nothing wrong with our house,' I said, 'and he loved your cake.'

'If he lives beyond the next stop he must've gone out of his way to come here.' Obviously Mum's imagination was working full time.

'Nonsense,' I said, in as firm and squashing a tone as possible. 'He always comes this way. His best friend's sister is a friend of Clary.'

'Oh, *Clary*,' said Mum. She likes Clary because it would be impossible to *dis*like her, but she feels more at home with Debs.

I sat down while a wave of complete helplessness swooshed over me. There was Mum, unconscious of the fact that I knew she had a secret, bustling happily between table and fridge, her henna'd curls catching the light. She was wearing her working uniform of jeans and a lavender linen pinnie she'd copied from an old dress of Grannie's, and, as I watched her, I wondered who she would've turned into if she'd stayed on at college and become a proper artist or designer or whatever. Of course, she'd never have met Dad and had Nairn and me, so I ought really to be grateful for the event that had propelled her out of one life and into another. But how different a person would she have been? Would she still have seen herself as not as good or as clever as other people?

'Rosa, if you've nothing better to do, you can help: all this has to go in the freezer. And as for you, Nairn, get out from under my feet.'

Nairn grabbed a snack and cleared off, while I loaded the shelves and Mum started supper. Then, just when I thought that the subject of Andy was safely closed, she said, 'Did you say what that boy's surname was?'

'Byron, as in Lord, but he's no relation.'

'But he might be *distantly* related. And how old is he?'

'Oh, *Mum*,' I groaned. Now she was seeing him as an aristocratic cad, all ready to seduce Rosa, the innocent daughter of the people. A scenario, I realized, almost exactly like that of *Tess of the D'Urbervilles*, through which I was still struggling. 'You're as bad as Dad, you see everything as though it were some old book. Andy's just a *neighbour*, for heaven's sake. And don't ask me what his father does because his parents are divorced and I haven't been nosy enough to ask.'

'There's no need to take that tone. I was just taking an interest, like mothers are supposed to do.'

'Interest granted,' I said. 'There just isn't much to be interested in.' But even as I spoke, I knew that Mum wouldn't believe me. How could I possibly have a friend who looked like Andy without being interested?

I also wondered what her reaction would be if she knew who exactly Andy was. And Christabel's, once she realized that not only was the girl in the low-cut blouse the daughter of her old acquaintance, but that acquaintance was living just down the road?

'Rosa, if you're not going to help, you can just get out of my way.' Mum didn't sound cross, but was regarding me with a sly wee smile.

'Right. I'll go and do some homework then,' I said, and tramped off upstairs.

Once in my bedroom, I chucked my stuff down and pulled the curtains without looking out. Andy would be home by now. He wouldn't tell Christabel who my mother was, would he? Of course not. He'd probably forgotten our conversation already. He'd be thinking about the friend to whom he'd asked to be remembered. Why ever had I let Clary come home with me on the bus? Why hadn't I realized there was a chance of her meeting Andy? Debs would never have made a mistake like that.

At the thought that I was comparing myself unfavourably to Debs, world leader in teasing and flirting, I did give a howl – but a small, restrained one. Then I unclipped my hair and did it up again into a tight, old-lady knot, just to prove to myself that I was never, ever going to indulge in all that eyelash-fluttering stuff. And finally I fetched the tarot book and sat down on my bed. First things first. Before I could confront all the other problems and mysteries that the cards had brought down on me, I had to succeed as Gypsy Zerlina.

I took the cards out of their new hiding place at the bottom of my biology folder and laid them out on my patchwork bedspread. Mum had made this for me when I was about eight, and I'd never had the heart to tell her it was getting a bit babyish for a teenager. The cards, however, seemed to like it. The faded colours of the old pack blended perfectly with the soft fabrics that Mum had chosen, and watching the pictures sift down through my fingers, I began to feel more confident. I could do this. The meanings of the individual cards were becoming clearer and clearer to me. I paused, the next card in the fan poised between my finger and thumb. 'What's going to happen at the fair?' I whispered. I let it fall, face up, into place.

A woman sat on her bed, bent over in despair, her face buried in her hands. Behind her, nine swords barred the way. The bed was covered with a patchwork spread.

CHAPTER eighteen

'So how does it feel to see your name in lights?'

I turned from contemplating the poster which the art department had made for my booth – GYPSY ZERLINA, SEER TO THE STARS, PSYCHIC SATISFACTION GUARANTEED – to find Clary standing behind me, her arms, as usual, full of books. Except that these were for the stall she was helping to run on the other side of the school hall. It was ten minutes before the doors were due to open for the fair, and kids were running about in an enjoyable panic.

'You certainly look the part,' Clary continued. It was hard to tell if this was a compliment, as Debs and Leanne had got me dolled-up in a fringed shawl and flouncy skirt and scary amounts of green eyeshadow, scarlet lip gloss and peach blusher. But at least the blusher was hiding the fact that I was white with terror – a fact I certainly wasn't going to reveal to Clary.

'Thank you, fair lady,' I said. 'May fortune smile upon you.'

'I think you'll need fortune's smiles more than I will. All I've got to do is sell books; you've got to give psychic value for money.'

'It'll be easy,' I said brightly. Inside, however, I felt terrible. The prospect of reading the cards had been bad enough before I'd asked them my foolish question, but now that I'd had an answer, I would willingly have been stabbed with one of the nine predicted swords rather than go through with the afternoon's performance.

'I bet you'll make more than we do, no matter what you tell your clients. Just look at the rubbish I've got to unload!' And sneering at her armload of sagas and thrillers, Clary eddied away to her stall. 'Good luck!' she called over her shoulder, and something else which I missed because Debs grabbed me, exclaiming, 'Rosie! Get into your booth! The door'll open in a minute and you don't want people to see you – it'll spoil the mystery.'

If I felt plain daft in my gypsy outfit, Debs was obviously revelling in hers. She was wearing a black satin bodice from Ann Summers, boned, laced and very low cut, a crimson flamenco skirt and huge hoop earrings. She had also slathered herself with instant tan. I was so overcome by her appearance that I allowed her to push me into my tent, where the cards were waiting for me on a little table draped with a silk shawl.

I sat down in the chair opposite the one where, in a few minutes, my first client would sit, and picked up the cards. I'd been afraid the pack would be unwilling to appear in public; that the cards would fool me by being either stiff or slippery in my hands; but, on the contrary, they seemed to feel far more lighthearted about the adventure than I did. They positively frisked through my fingers, as though they couldn't wait to get started. Of course, I realized that think-ing about the pack in this way was sheer imagination, but I couldn't help attributing a personality to them. For instance, I'd been tempted to slip the really heavy cards – Death, the Tower, some of the Swords – out of the pack for the after-noon so that I'd be spared giving anyone bad news, but the whole pack had gone sullen, and the cards had clumped together as though they refused to be separated.

Anyway, once I had the cards in my hands, I felt very slightly better. I'd make myself forget my fears, and concen-trate on being a genuine fortune-teller.

And as the afternoon went on, I hardly had time to worry. Largely due to Debs's efforts, I had an absolute flood of clients.

'Roll up, roll up for an immaculate reading from Gypsy Zerlina! A genuine Romany tarot reader is here, for one day only, to reveal what Fate has in store for you! Guaranteed one hundred per cent accurate, all proceeds to the children's hospice.'

It should've been hard, reading fortune after fortune without a break, but what I couldn't foresee, I simply made up. I gave girls glimpses of romance and excitement, and to older women I promised foreign travel, money and some good news concerning the family. I even got a few lads, urged on by giggling mates, and they were delighted to be told that a succession of conquests – I hinted at both sport-ing and sexual – lay ahead.

Of course, what made my task even simpler was that it was painfully easy to read the reactions of my customers. If

I was wrong, they looked bored or fidgety, but whenever I hit on something that was correct, they sat up straighter and focused more intently on the spread. So I'd elaborate on my hunch, guided by the signals given off unconsciously by my clients. Yet even as I did this, now and again I'd get a flash of pure intuition. A picture would appear in my head, something quite bizarre, like a palm tree, or a woman with long black hair walking down a gangplank. In this way I foretold some things that were completely true, like a visit to North Africa, and the arrival of a sister who never travelled by plane. Whenever this happened, I'd feel a small shudder inside, but it was a shudder of excitement.

By the end of the afternoon I was completely exhausted, but the people kept on coming.

'Just one more,' I said to Debs, as she swept open my curtained doorway to usher in another client.

'This lady is the last to be fortunate enough to consult Gypsy Zerlina,' said Debs, winking at me. 'Alas, the fair is over for this year, and we Romanies will be moving on to our next resting place.'

Behind Debs I could see that the fair was, indeed, almost over. The other stalls were closing down, and the jannie, who, as with every other school in the entire world, is the most important person in it, was hovering at the hall door with the keys in his hand.

'You are lucky indeed,' continued Debs to my client, a mousy, twenty-fivish woman. 'Let Gypsy Zerlina reveal your Fate.' And after showing her in, Debs retreated, presumably to fling herself all over Franklin, who had been challenging little kids to beat him at basketball.

I sneaked a long look at my final customer as I shuffled the cards. Too old to be a student, too young to be the mother of a pupil, she had long, not-very-clean hair clipped back at the side like a fifties film star and painted, bitten nails. Someone who usually takes care of her appearance but is currently too depressed to bother, I decided. And her shabby but classic coat and unpolished shoes told the same story. I was getting good at this. The cards flew through my fingers. I hadn't realized how sharp the edges were, but as I dealt out my last spread of the afternoon, I noticed a line of paper cuts down the inside of my index finger. But, of course, I reasoned, I'd never read for so long before. My hands would toughen up with practice.

I watched them as I placed the cards in a cross on the lilac silk shawl, admiring the confidence with which they now moved. The woman was watching as well, with complete concentration.

You'll have to be careful with this one, Rosa, I said to myself. And then I turned the spread over.

It was terrible. Worse than Marisa's. Every card showed a despairing, solitary figure. A woman with bandaged eyes, a man setting out on a lonely, moonlit journey and, worst of all, the same anguished woman sitting up in bed that I'd drawn on Thursday night. I stared at the cards in an absolute panic. All my usual speeches about not taking the cards at face value and searching instead for the symbolic meaning had deserted me. I glanced across at my client, and saw in her eyes such a look of misery, as though this were exactly what she'd expected, that I launched into my spiel, determined to uncover whatever tiny nugget of hope might lie concealed in the spread.

I began with the lonely woman in the garden, which had appeared in Marisa's spread, but whereas Marisa could look forward to moving into a future garden where she'd be playing with laughing children, this poor woman was fenced in by the stern King of Swords and his malevolent Queen.

'This card shows that you're most at ease when you're alone,' I began, with as much confidence as possible. 'Especially when you're using that time to create something.' There was a smudge of paint on her left hand. 'Perhaps painting.'

The quality of her silence altered, grew even more intense. I was on the right track.

'But you feel your privacy is being threatened by relatives.' The cruel King and Queen. 'These family members are putting their own interests before yours,' I continued. Perhaps I could gloss over all these swords. Perhaps I could make it sound less bad than it looked. But it was hopeless. As I spoke, my head began to fill up with pictures: the young woman in a hospital bed, bandages on her wrists; in tears while a man in horn-rimmed glasses shouted at her; walking around and around a little patch of grass, watched by a nurse.

As I told her what I saw, I tried to make it all sound more hopeful. Possibly a stay in some sort of retreat, a place with a garden where she could collect her thoughts and meditate, but as I spoke, I realized that she was looking at me with a mixture of pity and contempt, as though I were the one who was going mad. She knew perfectly well what I could see because she saw it herself, and she despised me for not telling her the truth.

I came to a halt before I reached the final card, and our eyes met. Then she got up and left.

I had never been so glad to come back and find the house empty. There were two notes on the kitchen table: one from Mum, saying that I was to make myself something from the freezer as she and the boys would stop off for a pizza on the way home, and the other from Dad, saying he'd gone to Callum's. So I made a mug of blackcurrant tea and slumped down at the table.

I didn't deserve anything nice or lucky to happen to me ever again. All I deserved was to go on sitting in an empty room for the rest of my life, listening to the rain on the window and eating frozen food. I laid the embroidered bag down in front of me and stroked the elderly velvet with one finger. I'd made someone who was miserable and ill even worse, and all through my stupid vanity. I was a silly, vain bisom, far worse than Debs. She'd just wanted to look pretty for Franklin, but I'd wanted everyone to admire my cleverness and my unlikely skill.

Daft bitch.

Eventually I raised my head from my hands and focused on the kitchen clock. It was an old wooden one in a glass case which made a friendly tick-tock, but now it seemed to be glowering at me and repeating, 'Daft bitch, daft wee bitch.' I wiped my eyes so that I could see the time more clearly and came back to earth. It was somehow almost 8 p.m.; I'd been sitting there for an hour, so it was a wonder that Mum hadn't come home and found me in this dismal heap, with the cards in front of me. I dragged myself up and padded stiffly into the hall. As I'd come in the back door, the rest of the house was in darkness. I switched on the light and made for the staircase. Perhaps I'd just go to bed and claim to be exhausted after a long afternoon of serving teas and counting change.

There was a flyer or something on the floor under the letter box, so I automatically scooped it up and aimed it at the hall table. We were too far out in the sticks to get the normal replacement-windows rubbish, so I glanced at it – and saw my name. It wasn't a flyer. It was a genuine letter, in an envelope, with my name scrawled across it in black biro.

Despite my guilt and desolation, my heart gave a huge, painful thump. There was only one person out here in the wild woods who could possibly be writing to me. But why would Andy *write* to me? It could only be because he wanted to say something which would be too difficult in person or over the phone – except, of course, he didn't have my mobile number. He'd never asked and I hadn't liked to offer. I remembered him pocketing Clary's card, and tore the envelope open.

Inside was a sheet of lined A4, torn out of a notebook.

Hey, Rosa,

How was it, being a gypsy? Why don't you skive off Monday afternoon, meet me 2 p.m. Filmhouse café?

Andy

I stared at the letter for quite a long time. It was the very first I'd actually had from a boy (not counting laddish texts) and it wasn't exactly romantic or inspiring, but I still clutched it to my gypsy blouse as I went up to my room. Once inside, the door safely shut, I looked at it again. Certainly not romantic, but downright mysterious. Skive off school? Was Andy so desperate to see me – or did he have something to – to – impart to me? I didn't know where that fancy word had come from, but it was what I felt.

I sank down on the bed. Good things couldn't possibly happen to me after what I'd done at the fair, and so Andy's blunt little letter felt like a bad omen. I dropped it, along with the cards, onto the patchwork spread.

Never again, I promised myself and Mum and anyone who might be listening out there in the unknown tarot world. I'll never tell fortunes again.

Never never never.

CHAPTER nineteen

When I trailed into school on Monday morning, I was horrified to find myself the centre of attention. I had a crowd of girls around me before I'd even reached the main entrance.

'Rosa, you were dead right about my mum's fortune! You said she'd get news from a distant land, and, when we got home, my auntie phoned from Australia!'

'Rosa, I was doing teas, so do mine at break, yeah?'

'I couldn't come on Saturday, so do mine too, please!'

'And mine!'

Every eager plea pierced like one of the fatal swords.

'Nah, that was it,' I said. 'The one and only appearance of Gypsy Zerlina. She's left with her caravan. For ever.'

'She doesn't mean it,' said Debs, pushing her way through my fans. 'She's just winding you up.'

'I do so mean it!' Who did Debs think she was, carrying on as though she knew me better than I did myself? 'I just did it the once, for the hospice.'

'Och, Rosa, I'll give the hospice a fiver!'

'So will I!'

Debs's eyes were gleaming. 'Think how pleased Mrs Grier would be, Rosie. You could all come back to mine and—'

'If Rosa says no, she means it.' Clary had appeared on the edge of the crowd, playing her usual role of my good angel. 'I dare say her parents don't like her doing it, isn't that right, Rosa?'

I nodded gratefully. 'Yeah, Mum doesn't really approve. Like I said, it was just because Mrs Grier asked me.'

There was a bit of muttering, but I shoved the others aside and joined Clary. She looked at me with raised eyebrows.

'Yes,' I said. 'Newsflash. The one and only Gypsy Zerlina renounces her psychic heritage.'

Clary gave what was, for her, a broad grin.

'Once was enough,' I continued, 'so you can smirk as much as you like.'

'I'm not smirking.'

'You are too.' And now I came to think of it, Clary did seem a shade less serious than usual, although the huge difference in her appearance was that instead of a plait, she was wearing her hair loose. It spilled down over her shoulders like golden syrup off a spoon.

'In fact,' I said, 'it's not *all* down to your good influence that I've decided not to pursue a lucrative career as a gypsy.'

'I don't care who it's down to,' she said primly, 'as long as you've given up.'

'Oh, it's definite.' Wandering along the corridor to our

first class didn't seem the ideal time to embark on the terrible saga of my final reading, so I asked the usual Monday question. 'So what did you do at the weekend? Apart from sell books.'

Clary looked modestly downward. 'Oh, the usual, you know. Homework, lunch at the grandparents'.'

I studied her more carefully, and she tilted her head so that her curtain of hair swung between us.

'So why did you lose the plait?' I said, as casually as possible. 'I mean, it looks great, but you've always had plaits.'

'There's no rule says I've got to look the same for ever. I'm defying expectations.'

'Mm, yeah.'

That was the sort of thing Andy would say.

I'm not a person who normally bunks off school – apart from PE, of course, which doesn't count. In fact, I'd say that missing PE is the duty of every thinking person. Even Dad agrees, despite actually being a teacher, and he only pretends to be cross when I've got into trouble for my mysterious disappearances. And by a weird – possibly even psychic – coincidence, the place to which Clary and I usually disappeared was my current destination, Filmhouse, where we either had coffee or watched obscure foreign movies. I liked these films, because, although I didn't always understand them, they somehow belonged to me. They were nothing to do with folk music or English literature or interior dec or any of the stuff my family enjoyed. They felt like my own country.

Today, however, scurrying down Lothian Road instead of heading obediently into modern studies, I was experiencing so many emotions I could hardly breathe. I was going to meet Andy, which ought to have been good, but then there was Clary's strange behaviour, which might be bad. And there was the fair, which I still couldn't bear to think about, and *why* did Andy want to meet me . . . By this time I'd reached Filmhouse, so taking deep, calming breaths, I scooted into the toilets, where I knotted up my hair and dabbed on some lipstick. My reason for doing this, I assured myself, was so that I'd look more like a student than a truant, and had nothing to do with impressing Andy Byron.

When I was as satisfied with my appearance as I'd ever be, I went through to the café and, standing on the top step, looked down into its deep blue interior. Andy was sprawled on one of the corner seats, smoking and wearing his trade-mark leather jacket.

'Surely you don't go to school like that?' I said. 'I thought your privileged establishment was uniform only?'

'Who's saying I've been to school?'

I remembered our first meeting on the bridge. 'So do you make a habit of it, skiving?'

He looked at me. 'And why not? That's what I think half the time, why bother? After all, if I can't go away and leave Christabel, what's the point in school?'

I stared back, and for a second I could see how he'd look when he was old, and the faint lines around his eyes and mouth had deepened.

'Or sometimes,' he continued, 'I think the opposite. I mean, leaving her would be like chucking a baby into the sea and hoping it can swim, but it might actually be the right thing to do.'

'Oh.' I sat down, not next to him on the sofa, as I would have liked, but opposite, on a bendy chair. 'Oh, Andy.' All my own worries dwindled by comparison. 'But don't you have any relatives, or family friends, or anything?'

'I told you, Dad's dug into East Sussex with his new family, Christabel's parents live in Sutherland and they're about eighty, and as batty as she is, and she's lost touch with most of her friends, apart from the infamous Fay—'

'The who?'

'Don't you want some coffee or something?'

'Oh yeah, I suppose.' I realized that I probably had far more money for snacks than Andy did, so I said, 'Can I get you something?'

'Just a coffee. Black.'

'So predictable.' I got back to my feet, went to the bar and bought a couple of coffees and a big slice of Death by Chocolate. I put the plate down in front of Andy and watched him unfold very slightly from the banquette. Boys are such simple creatures. Andy's problems might be worse than mine, but I wouldn't be cheered up by mere cake, no matter how fantoosh a name you gave it. In fact, I'd barely been able to eat all weekend, and the only reason Mum hadn't noticed was because Nairn had won first prize in his fiddle class, and the McBride family had been officially given over to rejoicing.

'Not as good as your mum's, but it still fills that gap,' said Andy, mouth already full.

Don't bother to say thank you, I thought. But perhaps it was embarrassing, being bought food by a girl. That seemed a kinder way of looking at it, so I gave a smile of Claryish radiance, took off my jacket and sank down – gracefully, I hoped – beside him. I'd abandoned my old T-shirt and was wearing a black top of Mum's which could be pulled down off the shoulders. 'Day to evening', as she called it. I'd left it in day mode.

'Thank you, Rosa,' said Andy, giving a wolfish, chocolate grin.

'Don't mention it.' I sipped my coffee, wondering why I was here and if this was actually a date.

'So what happened?'

'Sorry?'

'At the fair. Were your customers demanding their money back?'

'Not at all. They were lining up in droves. It was easy-peasy.'

'Really?'

'Really.' I scooped some foam off my coffee. When he didn't reply, I looked up and saw his expression of total disbelief. 'OK, there was one tricky one. And I made a mess of it. Satisfied?'

'You had one of your famous bridesmaid's dress visions? But black?'

I nodded, speechless. How did Andy manage to know so much about me?

'So there is something in it?'

'Yes, but Clary was right. I'm not doing it again, so let's just leave it, OK?' My eyes felt suspiciously hot.

'Sure.' Andy gave me such a kindly look that I very nearly did cry.

'You know,' I said quickly, 'there's been huge excitement chez McBride this weekend. Nairn won the fiddle prize.'

'That's handy. Your mum won't interrogate you about the fair.'

'Absolutely. She was too busy baking violin-shaped cakes and phoning Grannie and Danielle and Becky and Zara.'

'Who?'

'Mum's best friends.'

'Three best friends? She's lucky.'

This reminded me of something. 'Wait – didn't you say your mother only had one friend left?'

'Yes, Fay.' Andy stabbed his fork at the last morsel of cake. 'They were at art college together.'

'What?' I could actually feel my brain working. If my head had been sliced open, you'd have seen all the wee cells jostling one another as they passed the information along. 'Then she might know what all the mystery's about?'

'She might.'

'But what do you care? You said I should just leave it.'

'Well, when I got back from yours the other night, I asked Christabel what all the fuss had been about Natasha Munro – don't worry, I didn't say she was your mother or that I'd met her or anything – and she just clammed up.

So I asked again and she said it was none of my business, it had all happened so long ago, blah-blah, and it was only a tiff which she and Natasha had over a boyfriend.'

'*What?*' I couldn't control my face, which was setting into an open-mouthed mask of astonishment. 'I can't believe it – our mothers fighting over some man? I mean, they've got nothing in common.'

'I don't know. Good-looking, intelligent, talented – just like their offspring.'

'This is just so mad.' I was still too amazed to react to what might also have been a compliment. 'I don't suppose she said who this man was?'

'No chance. She shut up after that.'

'Do you think he might've been involved in the accident?'

'Don't know. But Christabel's got me curious as well now.'

'And you think perhaps her friend Fay . . .?'

'Yes. She owns the gallery where Christabel sells her stuff, and if there's one thing she likes, it's a bit of gossip.'

'So she mightn't be able to resist spilling some beans?'

'Just one or two. And I thought that we could pay her a little visit this very afternoon.' And he leaned back, looking infuriatingly pleased with himself.

'So what are we waiting for?' I was already on my feet. 'Where is this place? What's it called?'

'So aren't you going to say, "Thank you, Andy, for changing your mind and giving me this valuable information"?'

I was stotting up and down with impatience. 'Of course I'm grateful – thank you, Andy.' Whatever I'd expected from our meeting, it hadn't been this. 'C'mon, where are we going?'

'It's in the New Town; it's called Perfect Piece, P-I-E-C-E.'

'Yeugh.'

'I know.'

'So what's she like then, this Fay? Apart from being a gossip?'

'What d'you think? She's like someone who thinks it's brilliant to make puns.'

By now we were crossing the foyer, and I remembered something I'd meant to ask earlier. 'Why did you say to meet in Filmhouse?'

'Oh, I come here all the time: if anyone wonders why you're not in school, it's because you're working on your film-history project.'

I almost said it was amazing he'd never seen Clary and me, but then I thought that if I did, from now on he'd be searching the café for her lovely, glimmering hair, so I kept quiet and followed him out into the cold grey street.

CHAPTER twenty

Fifteen minutes later, having steamed across Princes Street and George Street, we were heading down the hill and into the New Town – so-called only because it's less old than the Old Town. On either side of us were elegant Georgian terraces, now converted into offices or flats, and, at ground level, chic little galleries or boutiques. Perfect Piece was a typical example. The stonework was painted a very fresh cream, the woodwork Mediterranean blue, and a single, curvy glass sculpture stood in the window. When we entered, a woman looked up from her desk at the back of the low, perfectly lit space, looked again, and then came towards us, her whole face gathered up into a pucker of surprise.

'Andy!'

'Good afternoon, Mrs Dalhousie, how are you?' Andy's expensively acquired charm and self-possession were given another outing. 'This is my friend Rosa. We wondered if we could have a word with you – no, Christabel's fine,' he said, as anxiety replaced the woman's initial surprise. 'We wanted to ask you something.'

'Well?' she bestowed a gracious, I'm-waiting-dear smile upon me. She was a small woman with a dieter's skinny face and a mass of immaculately streaked blonde hair, of which Mum would've approved.

I had so little idea how to start that I decided to jump right in. I tried to take a deep breath, but my ribs were mysteriously immobile, and I could only manage a gasp. 'Mrs Dalhousie, I don't think you recognize me, but I'm Natasha Munro's daughter. Perhaps you remember her from college?'

Like Christabel before her, although with less drama, Mrs Dalhousie fell back, one hand rising to flutter over her ruched jersey tunic. 'Natasha Munro! Wonders will never cease! You don't go to school with Andy, do you?' And she peered at me disbelievingly from between her spiky black eyelashes.

'No,' I said stiffly. 'We're neighbours.'

'Those little houses on the main road?'

I could feel myself turning red. When the revolution came – a student fantasy of Dad's – she'd be first against the wall.

Andy, however, had stepped in smoothly once again. 'Oh no, Rosa's family don't live on the *main* road; we met because we both walk home across the river, so imagine how surprised we were when we realized our mothers had been students together.'

'Well, of course, Christabel and I didn't really *know* Natasha, she wasn't one of our crowd.' I bet she wasn't, I thought. 'So I don't quite know what you want to talk to me about.'

However, as she said this, her eyes were almost triangular with anticipation. She knew fine well what we were going to ask. I was certain of it.

'The thing is, Mrs Dalhousie,' I said carefully, 'neither my mother nor Andy's are very keen on talking about it, but we know that something happened involving them both, an accident, or – or a quarrel, and we thought . . . Andy and I thought' – I looked from Andy to Mrs Dalhousie, whose eyes were growing brighter by the second – 'that you could throw some light on it. I mean, it's a bit silly, them not speaking after all this time, and being Andy's mother's friend, you must know everything. You could help sort things out.' I hoped that was enough flattery.

It wasn't.

'Oh but really, my lips are sealed! If your mother's moved on and doesn't want to discuss her past, I'm sure that's all for the best. I wouldn't dream of saying a word.'

She was enjoying herself so much that I longed to brain her with one of the swirly bits of glass that stood about the gallery.

Andy touched my arm very lightly – just a brush of the fingertips. 'Christabel did let slip something. She mentioned that she and Rosa's mother fell out over a boyfriend. Was that the big mystery?'

Mrs Dalhousie gave a tinkly little laugh, shaking her head so that her blonde locks rippled. 'If you wanted information on that point, you'd really have to ask Fergus himself.'

'Who?'

'Why, yes, dear,' she said, using 'dear' in that especially patronizing grown-up way. 'Your mother's old boyfriend Fergus McDonald.'

I didn't want to say 'who' again, like an owl, and give away the fact that Mum had told me nothing at all about her life pre-Dad, so I said, 'Oh, Mum had lots of boyfriends.'

'Or Fergie Mac, as he's known nowadays.'

'*Fergie Mac?*' I could only stare at her.

'You didn't know that Natasha used to go out with the great Fergie Mac?'

'The who?' It was Andy's turn to hoot.

I knew I must have looked totally glaiket, but I just couldn't get another word out. Once upon a time Mum, *my mother*, had been *Fergie Mac's girlfriend*.

'Who's Fergie Mac?' repeated Andy.

'Don't you know anything?' I snapped. 'The fantastically well-known folk singer of yesteryear.' And not only the fantastically etc. but one of Dad's mighty musical heroes. Did *he* know that Mum and Fergie Mac . . . ? I wished I could sit down. And Mum still played Fergie Mac's music – when we'd been painting together she'd actually been singing along.

'Oh yes, Fergus would be your man,' Mrs Dalhousie was saying, her eyes never leaving my face. I guessed she was torn between the pleasure of teasing me with snippets of information, and her loyalty to Christabel.

'And where is he now?' I demanded – although without much hope of getting an answer. I knew that he hadn't recorded in ages, so he might well have retreated to some distant heathery shore like Mull or Lewis.

'He could be anywhere,' said Mrs Dalhousie, confirming my suspicions. 'He used to be based in Edinburgh, but he hasn't done much recently, hitting the bottle again is what one hears, so it would be best not to go raking up the past in *that* direction.'

So why did you tell us about him? I thought. It was easy to answer my own question: because you just couldn't resist it, you rotten wee mixer.

'So all in all, Andy, I believe your mother is absolutely right not to want to keep looking backwards. You should respect her wishes. And Natasha's, of course.'

Mrs Dalhousie said this with an insincere smile larded over her face. I could hardly wait to get out of her poncy gallery.

'Well thank you very much, Mrs Dalhousie, for your valuable time,' I said, backing towards the door.

'Not at all – dear. And do give my very best wishes to Natasha. What did you say she was doing these days?'

'She runs her own business,' I said.

'Design,' said Andy.

'Oh.' Mrs Dalhousie paused, looking up at us and giving the small-person impression of being on tiptoe. 'Oh well, lovely to see you, Andy. Do look in any time you're passing, love to Christabel and tell her I'll see her very, very soon.'

'Goodbye, Mrs Dalhousie, thanks again,' said Andy, ushering me out of the gallery and down the stone steps to street level. If I hadn't been aware of Mrs Dalhousie watching us from behind the glass spiral, I'd have sunk to the pavement. Instead, I tottered to the next-door boutique (Suki Clothes for Kids) and sat down on the steps.

'I don't believe it. It's simply impossible – Mum and Fergie Mac!'

'Why's it so impossible?' Andy sat down beside me. 'And who did you say he was? I've never heard of him.'

I waved my hands. 'Where've you been? You don't have to be a folky to have heard of Fergie Mac. He was huge until about seven years ago. Singer-songwriter, ochone the glens, farewell the Clyde, that sort of stuff.' I stopped waving my hands and put my head down between them instead. 'I just don't *get* it. Dad's got all his albums; he says Fergie could've been the Scottish Bob Dylan with better marketing – and Mum went out with him and she *never said*.'

'Unless Fay's making the whole thing up.'

'She wasn't. She was having so much fun, leading us on. She could've told us loads more if she hadn't been afraid of annoying your mother.'

'She wouldn't need to worry about that. Christabel depends on her too much for selling her stuff.'

'Is that why they're friends? I mean, Fay's a total bitch, in case you hadn't noticed.' Guys are so easily taken in by wee women looking up at them.

'Oh, but I had. Only they didn't just go to college together; they went to the same boarding school.'

'You mean, best pals since their merry pranks in the dorm?'

'Yeah, and despite everything Fay has stuck by

Christabel. She still visits when all her other friends have given up on trailing out to Drumglass.'

'But it's just too weird to take in.' I'd reverted to Fay's bombshell. 'Mum didn't just go to art college, she went out with this famous guy. Well, famous in Scotland.'

'But was he famous at the time?'

I did a bit of mental arithmetic. 'No, it must've been before his first album – but, all the same, if I'd gone out with someone who became massive later on, you can bet I'd at least mention it every so often.' Then I realized what I'd just said. I'd mentioned 'going out' when Andy and I weren't exactly . . . I got to my feet. 'That stone is just too cold to sit on. Let's have more coffee.'

'OK.'

'Uphill or down?'

'Up, definitely. Down's too near my school.'

We headed back towards Princes Street, walking slowly because I was still too astounded to walk fast. Mum was shape-shifting before my very eyes, slipping out of her housewife clothes and emerging as someone far more exotic than even Gypsy Zerlina.

'It's not really so odd, you know.'

'What?'

'Your mum going out with this famous guy. I mean she's so beautiful.'

'What?' I said again.

'She's still glamorous now, so she must've been stunning in her teens.'

I was ashamed to say I'd never ever thought of Mum like

that. She is good-looking for a woman her age, and a lot more stylish, in her own bizarre way, than your average mum. But beautiful? If anyone was beautiful, it was Christabel with her classic bone structure.

I said so, but Andy disagreed quite vehemently.

'Christabel's a bit – I don't know what the magazine word would be – oh, unmoisturized, while your mum sort of glows and her hair's fantastic.'

The red hair which I hadn't inherited. I kept quiet.

'So it's hardly surprising, this Fergus wanting to go out with her. Boys were probably lining up. No wonder Christabel and Fay didn't like her.'

I kept sniffily quiet for a moment and then, when Andy didn't notice, I said, 'So the next thing is to find Fergus.'

Andy had slowed down to a dreamy saunter. 'How are you going to do that?'

I increased my pace. 'He might have his own website, and if he doesn't, his publishers will have one.'

'But if Fay's right and he's lying on the floor swigging Buckie, he's hardly going to be checking his e-mails.'

'That's Plan B. Plan A's to go round the pubs that hold folk sessions and ask where Fergus is holed up these days. Remember, Fay said she'd *heard* he was drinking again, so that means he's around somewhere, being gossiped about.'

'But hold it, Rosa. How'll we know which pubs?'

'Just follow Rosa, the girl detective. Dad's always going to gigs: we just need to check out his haunts.'

We had reached one of the islands in the middle of

George Street, and were standing under an immense statue of some VIP in a stone cape.

'But say we find him, what next? Are you sure you want to meet him?'

I turned on Andy. '*Of course* I want to meet him! And whose idea was it in the first place, interrogating Fay?'

'I didn't know what we were going to find out, did I? I thought the whole boyfriend thing was going to boil down to some girly tiff – mystery solved – but Fay was doing all this hinting, as though . . . as though your mother had something to be ashamed of.'

'So?' I plunged into the traffic and made it to the pavement, Andy at my heels. 'I don't believe for *one minute* that Mum did anything wrong. Something happened which upset her so much that *she* left college, remember, not your mother, and I want to find out what it was so that I can . . . can tell her I know, and then perhaps she'll talk about it. If she wants to. She could even go back to college.' I said all this at high speed, weaving between our fellow pedestrians.

Andy caught up with me at the next crossing and grabbed my sleeve. 'Rosa.' I stopped. 'Things don't always work out the way you want them to.'

Looking at his face, I realized that he'd had a lot more experience of things not working out than I had. I hesitated. 'But it's still worth trying.'

'And even if we find this Fergus, why should he speak up when no one else will?'

This had already occurred to me, but I shrugged like one

of my foreign-movie heroines. 'I'll use my feminine wiles on him.'

'Aye, right,' said Andy, sounding, for the first time ever, very slightly Scottish.

'Aye,' I said, taking off with a fresh burst of speed. 'Come on. Dad's howffs are all up The Mound.'

'What about that coffee?'

'*Mañana*,' I said, switching accents like a real detective.

One of my reasons for looking for Fergus in Edinburgh was down to a story called 'The Blue Bird of Happiness', which Dad used to read to me. In it, two children search far and near for this magic bird which, of course, turns out to be the actual wee bird they have in a cage at home. (This was obviously written pre-Animal Lib days.) So I reckoned that if Andy and I asked around Edinburgh, under our own noses, we'd turn up the old singer in a couple of choruses of 'Loch Lomond'.

And I was right.

In the first pub there was agreement that Fergus was very much around. He'd been seen in the Royal Oak the week before; he'd performed in Aberdeen; and there was talk of a new album with a young Spanish singer – so although he might no longer be a big star, he still had a loyal following. None of these followers, however, knew exactly where to find him.

The second pub was warm and dark and silent, the few customers slumped with their pints and their fags, each in a private dwam. The bartender gave us a wary look, but when I launched into a spiel about wanting to interview the renowned Fergie Mac for a student magazine, a big helpful smile pushed its way through his beard.

'Now he's very definitely at home because he was in here only a couple of days ago.'

'So he does live in Edinburgh?' I was hot on the trail!

'Oh aye, he'll be in the phone book.'

'But there could be dozens of F. McDonalds.'

'He lives in Stockie, somewhere near the river – that'll give you a lead.' He heaved a tattered phone directory onto the bar.

As I leafed through it, Andy leaning over my shoulder, one of the regulars perked up enough to take an interest in our quest. 'Aye, it's in Stockbridge ye'll find Fergus,' he said. 'My daughter lives down there, she says she's forever falling over him: he drinks all along Raeburn Place.'

This was hardly encouraging, but I'd found the entry. Fergus McDonald, at an address in St Stephen's Street, which is at the bohemian heart of Stockbridge.

'There you go!' I jabbed my finger triumphantly into the soft paper. 'I told you it would be easy, Andy.' I'd been a bit tired and footsore, but now I felt full of bounce and enthusiasm. I'd track down Mum's old boyfriend to his riverside den, shake the truth out of him, confront Mum, reconcile her to Christabel, and talk her into going back to college – and all before breakfast tomorrow!

I thanked the bartender effusively, copied the address and number, and then bought a couple of Cokes. Andy and I sat down in a dark corner.

'We can go right now. I'll phone Mum and say I'm at Clary's.'

'Wouldn't it be easier just to phone him – at least check he's in?'

I hesitated. 'But I'd have to explain who I am – and what if he doesn't want to see me? I'd rather go there and do it face to face. And he's as likely to be in now as any time. Go on, call Christabel and tell her you'll be late.'

'What makes you think we've got a phone?'

'Excuse me?'

'Not everybody in the developed world has a phone.'

I still didn't get it. 'But what about your mobile?'

Andy leaned back further in his seat. 'The Byron finances don't actually quite stretch to telephonic communication. And before you ask, no, I don't have e-mail either.'

I went hot. I knew Andy and Christabel were skint, but I didn't know *anyone* who didn't have your basic phone. I'd just assumed their poverty was that elegantly tatty sort which stops short of actual hardship.

'Uh – oh, OK,' I muttered.

'Don't apologize,' said Andy, with an exasperating smirk.

I realized that he was *enjoying* my discomfort, and snapped, 'I wasn't apologizing. It was a natural mistake to think that someone from your school with a trust fund would be festooned with gadgets.'

'In my case, no. It's the simple life chez Byron. No phone, TV, microwave – Christabel has a *wireless* and I've got some music stuff my dad gave me and that's it.'

'Fine, I get the point.' I'd decided that I wouldn't be embarrassed – and I'd also realized that if Andy didn't have a mobile, then it wasn't from him that Clary hoped to hear every time she checked her messages. I couldn't help giving a huge, inappropriate smile. 'So if you can't let your mother know you'll be late, will she worry?'

'She twitches.'

'OK then. And another thing, if you don't have a phone, Fay isn't going to be calling Christabel right now and telling her that I'm actually Mum's daughter.'

'Oh, don't worry – you can bet the Dalhousie SUV will be rumbling up to Drumglass in the next day or two. What did you expect?'

I didn't want to admit I hadn't thought through all the implications of talking to Fay, so I said, 'As Christabel never leaves home, it's not going to matter what she knows.' Of course, if Andy were planning on ever inviting me back to Drumglass, then it *would* matter – it was easier not to think about this. 'Look, I can't skive tomorrow, it's all stuff I need to do, but the day after's just PE. I'll go down to Stockie then, so don't worry if you can't come with me.'

'Oh, I'll come.' Andy stretched his long arms and legs. 'I never have stuff I have to do.'

'Suit yourself. When I've passed all my exams and I'm a top-earning whatever, I'll drop my spare change in your woolly hat.'

'Don't be so boring. My school isn't about work, it's about networking. I could leave with nothing but a module in woodwork and someone's dad would still find me a job.'

Andy had this effect on me that even as I looked at his long, stained fingers and wished that he would lean forwards and fold them around mine, I also longed to hit him with something slimy, like a dead fish or a slice of cold pizza. However, as I very much wanted him to come with me, I just said, 'That's great then. Where'll we meet?'

So we did a bit of forward planning, said goodbye to the friendly barman and hit the long, long trail to Burnshead.

CHAPTER twenty-one

'Here we are.' Andy took my hand, and I wished that I could concentrate on how that made me simultaneously melt and sizzle inside. However, the fact that what we were looking at was Fergus McDonald's subterranean lair took the edge off my romantic excitement.

It was early in the afternoon, and we'd once again walked down through the New Town after meeting in a café. Now we were at the very foot of the hill and peering over the railings at a basement flat. Unlike the others in this casually fashionable district, the courtyard wasn't tarted up with cream paint and tubs of evergreens. Instead the flagstones were mossy underfoot and the paintwork scuffed.

'C'mon,' said Andy. 'It's two o'clock. He'll be expecting us.'

Andy had pointed out how disappointing it would be if we trailed all the way down to Stockie and either found the old guy not at home, or passed out in a nest of empty bottles, so I'd phoned him, told my story about an interview and made an appointment. Fergus had sounded neither flattered nor surprised, although what had surprised *me* was his strong Highland accent, a rarity in Edinburgh.

And now I was on the actual point of meeting him. Dad's folk hero, Mum's old boyfriend, and the person who could, if he wanted, tell me about her lost, mysterious past.

'Right. Fine,' I said, venturing down the slippery steps. There was something about the occasion that made me want to use words like 'venture' or 'quest'.

Andy was behind me as I crossed the dark area and pressed the bell. I've always hated that moment between ringing the bell and waiting for the person inside to answer. When I was wee I used to imagine that a hairy paw would appear round the door, to be followed by a toothy muzzle and yellow eyes. Obviously I didn't believe this any more, but I couldn't help suspecting that the old folkster might prove to be a different sort of wolf.

Then the door opened, and there he was. I'd checked his photo on an old CD cover, and in the ten years or so since it had been taken Fergie Mac had changed, but not necessarily for the worse. His mane of hair was grey, as was his beard, and his face, with the handsome hooked nose, was lined – but the photo hadn't prepared me for his devastating sea-green eyes.

He stood within the door, in old cords and a hand-knit jumper, and looked at us. His gaze rested much longer on me than it did on Andy, and I saw that my intuition was correct, and that he still regarded himself as a charmer.

'Mr McDonald,' I began, 'I'm Rosa McBride. I phoned you about asking you some questions for—'

'That you did,' he said, in the stately, mannered voice I recognized from the phone, 'but I'm thinking there was something you didn't tell me. You're the picture of Tash Munro, for all you have not got her red hair.'

After Christabel's wild reaction to Mum's name, I'd been bracing myself for something dramatic from her old boyfriend, but, unlike Christabel, he made no gesture of either delight or alarm. Instead he gazed at me as though . . . as though I were, well, beautiful. Like Mum. And I gazed back, understanding how he had enthralled both women. It wasn't just that he was still attractive, in a craggy, old person way; he was looking at me as though he could actually *see* me. As though he were paying attention to me, and to no one else. The mystery was how Mum had ever torn herself away from those admiring, emerald eyes and settled for cuddly old Dad.

Then I realized that he was waiting for me to say something, so I stammered, 'Yes, I – I am Tasha's daughter, but I didn't say on the phone because, because I thought perhaps you mightn't want to see me if, if—'

'And why ever not? What nonsense have you been hearing about me? Och, I've none but sweet memories of your mother, Rosa! Come away in.' And he stepped back to allow us into the narrow hall.

His jumper, as I passed him, smelled of woodsmoke and spliffs. I couldn't help inhaling extra deeply, and he gave me a canny sideways smile.

'Sit yourselves down.' He waved us into his living room and towards a beaten-up leather sofa before sitting in a matching chair. It was obviously his special seat, being surrounded by drifts of music magazines, newspapers, notebooks, an ashtray and empty mugs – but no bottles. A guitar was propped up within reach, and there was a wood-burning stove, which partially explained the smell of his jumper. Otherwise the room looked as though money had once been spent upon it – the leather furniture, a furry carpet, two big bendy chrome lamps – but had long since settled, like its owner, into a comfortable relationship with its own scruffiness. One wall was taken up by shelves of vinyl, cassettes, CDs, DVDs, old reel-to-reel tapes and equipment for playing all of these, while under the window was a table with all the usual computer stuff plus an electronic keyboard. There was no sign of any female presence.

'You said your name was Rosa?'

'Yes.' I was wondering desperately how to begin. I'd been taken aback by his recognizing me straight away – and now here he was, asking the questions.

'Would that be Rosa for "Dark Rosaleen"?'

'Yes,' I said again, astonished. 'How did you guess?'

'Och, that tune was aye a favourite of your mother's. It takes no skill to guess.'

I remembered all the times Mum had told me about hearing 'Dark Rosaleen' played the night she met Dad. Did he know that she'd already heard it with Fergus?

'She and my father heard it at a concert the night they met,' I said, doing my very best to look Fergus in the eye.

'Och, no doubt, no doubt,' he replied, smiling again, as

he had when I'd sniffed the hash. Somehow I didn't feel at all cross or offended, as I would've done if Andy, for example, had given me that superior grin. Fergus had, in fact, now turned his attention to Andy, whom he was regarding with a puzzled air. 'And your name is . . . ?'

'Andy Byron, sir,' said Andy, doing his super-polite act.

Fergus nodded at the deference but, still seeming puzzled, said to both of us, 'And so how can I help you? Are you here upon your mother's recommendation?'

'No,' I said. 'No, the thing is, Mr McDonald, my mother never told me she'd even met you.'

'She never mentioned me?' Fergus looked childishly hurt, as though he couldn't imagine Mum never having boasted of knowing the Scottish folk hero.

'Not a word,' I said, adding quickly, 'But she listens to your music all the time.'

'Ach well.' He leaned back in his squishy chair. 'I suppose it is understandable.'

'And that's what I want to know about.' As he leaned back, I leaned forwards, perching on the edge of the engulfing sofa. 'You see, Mr McDonald—'

'Fergus, please.'

'Fergus, like I said, she and Dad have all your music, but she's never said she knew you, and she's never even said that she was at art college. I only found out recently. And now I know that she read the tarot and that there was some sort of accident, but she won't talk about it. And Dad won't either.'

'And so you think perhaps I will?'

I nodded, because it was hard to speak with those eyes fixed on me.

'And if your mother is silent, how did you find out so much?'

'We were moving house . . . and I found these.' I took the tarot pack out of my bag and held it out to him.

Fergus's expression altered, all the furrows on his face quivering and running together, as though at the mercy of some sci-fi special effect. Then he took the velvet bag from me and turned it over and over in his hands, smoothing his fingers along the embroidery, as I had done.

'I mind Tasha making that as though it were yesterday. I never thought I'd be seeing it again. She took it with her when she left.' And Fergus shook his head so sorrowfully that, despite his stagy, self-aware presence, I actually believed he was upset.

'Mum was angry when she saw me with them, so of course that made me curious—'

'And you've been more than curious, haven't you?' He'd fixed his green eyes on me once more. 'You've discovered that you have the gift, just like your mother.'

'I'm not sure I know what you mean.'

He shook his head again. 'You can read the cards and see into the future. I don't have the second sight myself, but it runs through my family, and so I know enough to treat it with care. Your mother, however, wouldn't listen to me. And you've been doing the same, haven't you, Rosa? Do I have to warn you into the bargain?'

If he didn't have the second sight, he had something very

close to it. 'No,' I said. 'No, I've learned my lesson already. You don't have to warn me.'

Fergus relaxed further back into his chair and smiled, and for an extraordinary moment I felt completely accepted and at peace. I smiled back.

'So, Rosa,' he said. 'Not only beautiful, but wise.'

Normally I'd have curled up with embarrassment at such flattery, but I just said, 'That's me.'

'However,' he continued, 'charmed though I am to make your acquaintance, you haven't yet explained how you come to be here.'

'I had the cards with me at Andy's one day, and his mother recognized the bag, and it turned out she'd been at art college with my mother.'

It was Andy's turn to be the object of Fergus's regard. 'So that's it! I knew your face, but I couldn't place it. You must be Christabel's son. A whole run of surprises.'

'Yes,' said Andy. 'We're neighbours, but our mothers haven't . . . bumped into each other.'

Fergus chuckled, and I suspected that he was amused to think of his two old girlfriends within a stone's throw of each other.

'It's not funny,' I said. 'Whatever it was that happened, it really hurt Mum.'

'Yes, Rosa, you are right, it is no laughing matter – but didn't your mother go back to college in Glasgow?'

'No. I mean, it's not as though she's sat around moping all her life – but . . . but I want to know what happened. You must see that.'

'Rosa,' said Fergus, 'I would help you if I could. But it's not my secret. If Tash won't discuss it, it's not my place to interfere.'

'Oh please!' I was almost in tears. How could I bear being so close to the truth without finding it out? I looked at Andy.

'It's knowing that there's a mystery,' he said. 'Rosa's mother, mine, Fay—'

'Now why am I not surprised to hear you mention Fay? She was aye a vindictive wee trollop; you could rely on her to put in a bad word for anyone. No doubt she took pleasure in informing you that I am an unregenerate drunkard, but I doubt if I put away as much of the hard stuff as she does the vodka.' He shook his head. 'So what else did she have to tell you?'

'Just hints. Hints that something awful had happened.'

Fergus gave a deep, deep sigh, and I sat forwards again, unconsciously clasping my hands. 'Please,' I said, 'please tell me. I'd so much rather know the truth than . . . than imagine things.'

'The truth!' said Fergus. 'It's been my experience that the truth is a highly overrated commodity.'

'Dad says – my father says that the truth sets you free.'

'Your father and I are at odds there.'

'Please,' I said again.

And then Fergus nodded, and I knew that I had won because, for an instant, he and I had both been thinking that, if things had been different, *he* might have been my father.

'Very well,' he said. 'I will tell you the truth and then you can judge who is correct, your father or me.' He ran his fingers over the velvet bag. 'I will have to tell you from the beginning.'

And I shuddered, but sat up straight.

CHAPTER twenty-two

'Now, when I met your mother, she was in her first year at college while I was in my final – I thought in those days that I would be a painter – and a very beautiful and fetching young woman she was. She had many admirers, and I think it would be fair to say that I was foremost among them.'

Fergus's lilting accent made their affair sound so ... so elegant that I longed for someone to feel that way about me. An *admirer* – that was what I wanted. I sneaked a look at Andy, but he was staring straight ahead.

'And one of Tash's many attractions was that she could read the tarot. There she'd be, laughing as she laid out the cards, as though telling a fortune were not a serious business. All the arts of divination require humility, and none more than the tarot. That was when I warned her – but would she heed me?'

Oh, Clary, I thought.

'Now one of the young fellows who fancied Tash was a lad named Sean Donnelly. He was always begging her to read his cards, but she refused because she knew he was in love with her and she suspected that he would take anything she told him to heart. However, one night at a party Tash gave in. She laid out the Celtic Cross' – that was the spread I'd taught myself – 'but card after card brought ill luck: swords, broken hearts, perilous journeys' – once again I saw the bitter, pitying eyes of my final client at the fair – 'and the final card, the crown of the cross, the last card that my poor Tash laid down was the Death card.'

Fergus paused dramatically, and I had the distinct feeling that this was far from the first time he'd told the story. Every word sounded sincere, yet there was a composed quality to his speech that made me imagine him, late at night, entrancing some other woman with this tale of a lost love – just as he was entrancing me.

'Up until then it had all been a game to her' – I could feel Andy looking at me, but I refused to look back – 'but now Tash sat and looked at the spread, and so did Sean, and it was nothing that he could have been anticipating. Even without knowing the meaning of each card, it was obviously a dire outcome! And our friends, meanwhile, had gathered around, every one of them fallen silent.'

I could see it clearly: Mum and Sean encircled by shadows, the fatal spread between them.

'But Tash did well: she went over the spread card by card, explaining how it was nothing like as bad as it seemed, and how it was a spiritual death followed by resurrection which the final card promised. Well, Sean seemed to accept it, but during the next few days there was a bit of whispering among those who had been there – and foremost among them, I'm sorry to say' – and he turned his mournful regard upon Andy – 'were your mother and her friend Fay.'

There was a short, fraught silence before he continued his tale. It was certainly a tale, a detached, Eng. Lit. part of my brain decided.

'And then, a few days later, a lovely summer morning, Sean was found dead on his kitchen floor.'

Andy and I both gasped, and Fergus raised and lowered his head in something too solemn to be called a nod.

'His flat had an old gas cooker, and Sean was lying beside it, one burner turned full on but unlit. He had the best part of a bottle of whisky inside him, and the police thought that he'd attempted to light the gas, but passed out before he realized that his match hadn't caught the burner. But the talk was that either he'd killed himself for love of your mother – or out of despair at the fortune she'd given him.'

'But it wasn't true?' I whispered.

'Not a word of truth in it! There was no suicide note, and if Sean had meant to kill himself, he was just the lad to leave a note: he would've sat up all night composing it! But dying cursed by unrequited love is a more romantic end than dying too drunk to light the gas, so people talked it up and made out that Tash had bewitched him.'

I had the oddest sensation that my *face* was cold, and I must've looked strange, because Fergus paused and then said, 'Rosa, I am upsetting you. Can I make you some tea? Or are you old enough for a real drink?'

'No,' I said. 'Go on. Please go on.'

'Very well. Now I am coming to something else unpleasant. A reporter from one of the tabloids had been nosing around, and someone told her the story of Tash's spread.'

Andy tensed beside me.

'I cannot say for sure who it was, but your mother, Andy, for all it may be hard for you to believe, had a wee fancy for me.' He knew perfectly well that I at least had absolutely no trouble in believing it. 'So, for whatever reason, it was she and Fay who were leaders in spreading the gossip against Tash. And you can imagine the item in the paper – no names, of course, but everyone knew it was Tash. Now, through all this terrible time I counselled her to keep quiet and hold on. She'd done nothing wrong, and by and by the whole dreadful affair would be forgotten. But Tash was beside herself. She wept and cried, said that she was to blame and that she should've listened to me. She almost got it into her head that she was a witch. Nothing I could say would comfort her. And then one day I came home from college and she was gone. Packed up and left. I rushed round to her parents' flat, and your grannie told me she'd gone to stay with relatives in Glasgow until things had quietened down.'

'But didn't you—?' I began.

'Och yes, I followed her. I pleaded with her to come home, but she plain refused. I can look back now and say perhaps I should've gone with her – but first it was my degree show, and then an agent had heard me sing and offered me a tour – and so the moment passed.'

For all his fine words, the moment had passed because he hadn't cared enough. That was what I thought as we sat in silence, the tale at an end.

'Rosa?' Fergus was speaking to me. 'I'll make that tea now.' He hoisted himself out of his chair – he could only have been Dad's age, but he moved like a much older man – and left the room.

Andy and I looked at one another.

'Well, Rosa,' he said, 'you got what you wanted.'

I wondered why he sounded bitter. My head felt so fuzzy that it was difficult to work things out, but then I got it. Clever Rosa. Of course, my mother had been foolish but innocent, while Christabel was guilty, at the very least, of malicious gossip; at worst of shopping Mum to the tabloids.

'Yes,' I said. 'Sorry. I understand. But perhaps Christabel wasn't the one who told—'

'But if she were, it would explain a lot.'

I nodded bleakly, and sank back into the sofa. 'Like why she was so horrified to see Mum's cards.'

'But she can't have felt as bad as your mother.' Andy put his arm round me. 'I'm sorry, Rosa.'

'So am I.' As I allowed myself to rest my head on his shoulder, I wondered if this quiet moment of leaning against him would ever happen again. After all, I was the daughter of the woman whom his mother had wronged – just like in one of Dad's daft old books! Then I wondered why I felt so tired. I could've curled up and fallen asleep. Fergus could cover us with sheets of his music – and then I remembered Mum singing along to a Fergie Mac album as we painted Nairn's room. I'd been sulking, not listening to the words properly; it had been some fairy story about a bird sewing, a red bird.

'You'll be ready for your tea now.' Fergus had entered with a laden tray, and I made myself leave the circle of Andy's arm to clear a space on a nearby table.

'Fergus,' I said, still half dreaming, 'you know that song of yours about a bird sewing—?'

'Ah yes!' Fergus lowered himself into his chair in the same careful manner as he'd got up. 'Whether you know it or not, when you refer to a young woman as a "bird" you are quoting an old Anglo-Saxon word meaning needle-woman. So my song is simply about a young woman who is embroidering. A woman with beautiful red hair.'

'Mum sings it.'

'Does she now? Then nothing is wasted.'

'Dad says you were the Scottish Dylan,' I said.

'A man of remarkable taste – but only to be expected.' And for a second I caught a glimpse of some genuine emotion on Fergus's face, but before I could identify it, it was gone.

'What nice cups,' I said brightly. And they were too: white with green rims and green saucers, much more stylish than I would've expected a lonesome male to possess.

'A gift. Now, Rosa, Andy, it's perhaps too early in the day for a wee dram – but a relish in your tea?' He held up a bottle which he'd brought in with the cups and teapot. 'Not of the most regal quality, I fear.'

Very few people actually say 'a wee dram', and of those

who do, Fergus is probably the only one who could get away with it. Andy and I both nodded, and Fergus poured and relished our tea. It tasted odd, but comforting.

'So, Rosa,' said Fergus, after we'd all sipped for a bit. 'Who was correct?'

'Sorry?'

'Your father or myself? Has the truth set you free?'

I put down my cup. 'No,' I said. 'You were right. But I'd still rather know the truth.' It wasn't so much that I hadn't been set free as that I'd been set free from not knowing, only to be burdened with knowledge.

Fergus was regarding me with so much sympathy that I wished I could look away. 'Yes, Rosa,' he said, 'you are braver than your mother. She was like a bird, sure enough. She wouldn't look at things. She panicked and flew away.'

I could feel tears running down my cheeks, and I buried my head in my bag while I rummaged for a hankie.

'Here.' Fergus handed me a box of tissues which he'd dug out from the heaps of stuff around his chair.

I took a handful and blew my nose and mopped my face.

'Don't mind crying,' said Fergus. 'After all, you took the courageous path. You could have chosen not to know.'

If Andy hadn't been there, I think I'd have had a proper weep, but with him beside me on the sofa doing a shifty, embarrassed, guy thing, I felt obliged to control myself.

'It's better knowing,' I said, as steadily as possible. I took a huge gulp of my whisky tea. 'I mean,' I continued more confidently, 'now perhaps I can do something.'

Fergus and Andy spoke together.

'And what exactly would you do?' said Fergus, and 'Haven't you ever heard of masterly inactivity?' said Andy.

'Well, the first thing is, I'll never read the cards again.' Fergus had laid them on the table beside the tea things, and now I picked them up. The velvet bag felt even warmer and more alluring after having been in his hands. 'Mum doesn't want them any more.' My voice was trembling. 'Won't you take them?' And I held them out towards Fergus. 'Please?'

He stretched his hand out, and for a moment we held the tarot pack between us. Then Fergus closed his nicotine-stained fingers around it, and my hand fell back, empty and cold, into my lap.

'Thank you, Rosa,' he said. 'I'll keep them safe. And I'll be glad to have a bit of your mother's embroidery by me.'

I nodded because I couldn't speak.

Andy, without being invited, poured some more whisky into his cup. 'So what else will you do?'

'Sorry?'

'First, and if you ask me, long overdue decision to give up the cards, so second . . . ?'

'I'm not sure. Tell Mum I know. Speak to her.'

Fergus sighed. 'And what would that accomplish?'

'She wouldn't have to keep hiding things. She could go back to college.'

'And what does she do now?'

'She's a home hairdresser. She goes round – oh, mostly old ladies, or mothers with young kids.'

'And isn't that a useful profession?'

'I suppose.'

'There are enough artists in the world without adding to them! And isn't she happy with your father and yourself and—?'

'My brother.'

'Ask yourself, would she be any happier if she knew that you knew her story?'

'Well, Rosa?'

With both Andy and Fergus looking at me, I couldn't find a sensible answer.

'But if I don't tell her, I'll be keeping a secret as well.'

'It was your choice, Rosa.' Fergus leaned back in his chair, the cards in his hands. He smiled at me, and reluctantly I smiled back.

'You win,' I said.

'So we will drink to secrets.' And he refilled our cups.

We all drank, and then Fergus asked how we'd first met, so we told him the whole story from Mum and Dad's party to the helpful barman.

'What a tale!' Fergus looked highly gratified at being the object of our quest. 'So your mothers are neighbours and have no idea of it? But surely it is only a matter of time before they meet.'

'Christabel doesn't go out much,' I said quickly. 'She has her work, and her garden—'

'She also has agoraphobia,' said Andy.

'Ah.' Fergus, I noticed, didn't seem surprised. 'Your mother, Andy, was a beautiful young woman, as lovely as Tash in her own way, but you'll forgive me if I say that there was aye something out of kilter about her. There was always the feeling that it wouldn't take much to send her over the edge.'

'I don't think Christabel's ill now because of what happened then,' said Andy stiffly. 'She always says how happy she was at college.'

'I didn't say it was a direct result,' said Fergus, 'but I would guess that she has had more to endure than most people.'

And I thought again about Christabel, digging alone in the rain, while Mum pluttered happily around Nairn's bedroom. And then I thought about Fergus watching Mum as she sewed.

'Do you ever still think about my mother?' I said.

'Och, Rosa!' he cried, raising his cup to me. 'I think about them all, every one! And from today, I'll think of you also.'

CHAPTER twenty-three

'What an old phoney!' said Andy.

We'd finally emerged from Fergus's flat, and I felt thoroughly disoriented. It had been bright and cold when we'd descended the steps, but now the day seemed to have dimmed into a misty gloaming.

'I liked him.' I balanced unsteadily on the kerb, blinking at the streetlights. 'There was something about him. He was – oh, you know, wild and cosy at the same time.'

'Obviously a ladies' man,' said Andy.

'What would you know about it?' I said, responding to his scornful tone. Yet I had to admit to myself that it was more than liking I felt for Fergus, and I had a sorrowful presentiment that I could spend the rest of my life searching for someone who would look at me as he had done.

'C'mon, Rosa, before we go home we need coffee.'

'I suppose.' Despite everything, I'd never before felt so warm and uncaring, and I wanted to stay this way. I made a graceful, expansive gesture. 'The quest has ended. Gypsy

Rosa has hung up her spangled shawl, and from now on she travels the road alone.'

I waited to hear what Andy would say.

'*Black* coffee.'

'Rosa, don't you dare tell me you skived off PE again! The school phoned; there was a message on the machine when I got back.'

Mum, lying in wait, strode through the kitchen door. She was wearing jeans, high-heeled boots and a laced suede jerkin, a Xena-style outfit which would've been scary in itself, without the hands on hips and flashing eyes with which she was confronting me.

'Sorry, Mum,' I said.

'Sorry's not good enough!'

'I won't do it again.'

'You won't get the chance, young lady! I've given the school secretary my mobile number so she can call me at once if there's any more of this nonsense.'

'It was only PE, for God's sake.'

I'd returned home overwhelmed by Mum's secret history and thus inspired to be all sorts of noble, old-fashioned things, like dutiful and obedient. Anything to make up for the harm that Christabel had done her – and here I was, just like on the first day at Burnshead, my resolution broken already! Worse than a daft bitch, a useless wee hoor.

'Don't take that attitude with me; I'm not your father. Schools are cracking down really hard on absenteeism. It'll be a black mark against you if you carry on like this.'

'A university's going to reject me because the PE department gives me a bad report? I don't think so.'

Good, self-sacrificing Rosa seemed to be standing halfway up the stairs, wringing her hands over the behaviour of sullen, teenage Rosa, who was posed defiantly in the kitchen doorway.

'And don't you talk back to me – I'm not having it.' Mum stamped over to the cooker and prodded something that was simmering in one of the pans on the hob. 'And just where did you get to for an entire afternoon?'

'I ran into Andy and we went for a coffee.'

'Did you arrange to meet him?' Clouds of steam were gushing around Mum, as though she were standing at the Hellmouth.

'Yes.'

'So you were with him all the time you should've been at school?'

I had such a strong sensation of no longer being myself that I sat down abruptly at the table. Cutting school to meet a boy was the sort of thing that Debs or Leanne would do, and I didn't feel guilty, as I should. And drinking whisky all afternoon with Mum's disreputable old boyfriend was even worse, and I didn't feel guilty about that either.

'Oh, Rosa!' Mum came and sat down opposite me, and I saw that Andy and Fergus were right. She was beautiful. The steam had made her hair frizzle up into hundreds of little curls, and her cheeks were tinged with pink. She looked as young as she must've been when she met Fergus. 'I know how infuriating it is when your parents worry about you, and I know that missing school once or twice doesn't seem so very bad – but Andy's older than you, isn't he? What's he doing roaming around town when he ought to be studying?'

I knew what she really meant. *Roaming around with my wee girl, leading her astray.*

'It was only this once.' And at the thought of how true this was, because we no longer had any reason to meet in secret, good Rosa stepped back into control. 'I'm really, really sorry, and I won't do it again.'

Mum's face softened. 'I'm sure Andy's a nice enough lad, but I reckon he's from the sort of family where you can get away with anything if you've been to the right school and know the right people. We're not like that, Rosa. Just get yourself into trouble – *any* sort of trouble, not the sort you think I mean – and sometimes you can never get clear of it.'

I stared at Mum. It was almost as though her old psychic skill had surfaced, and she knew intuitively what I'd been up to. I wanted so much to tell her that I knew everything, but Fergus was right. What good would it do after all these years?

I cleared my throat. 'I'm not going to do anything daft.'

'I should hope not. I should hope we've brought you up to know better.'

She was playing the family card, and I could feel myself beginning to feel guilty again. Guilty, and also a bit cross. She was making it so hard for me to do this dutiful stuff!

'I won't – I mean, you have. Honest.'

Mum didn't look totally convinced, and even when I offered to help with supper, she didn't chat or sing as she usually does.

If my supposedly having a wee coffee with Andy threw her into this state, what on earth would she do if she knew where I'd really been?

CHAPTER twenty-four

The next morning it was all I could do to crawl out of bed. I'd escaped a hangover, but somehow getting up and going to school seemed pointless. When all the adults in my life had made such a mess of things, why on earth should I follow their rules? However, I'd made promises to Mum and myself, so I scrambled myself together and went downstairs. She was too busy seeing Dad and Nairn off to notice how pale I was, and instead of being thankful to avoid questions, I felt resentful and disappointed.

After a quick cup of coffee I left the house and slithered down the track towards the bus stop. It was a beautiful morning, like the one when I'd first seen Andy but colder, and the leaves were now lying in crisp shoals under my feet. I was almost tempted to forget everything – promises, resolutions, parents – and stay in the woods all day. I'd actually stopped, with my hand on the sunny side of a silver birch, when I heard someone call my name.

I turned to see Andy plunging after me.

'Aren't you going to be late for school?' He usually left earlier than me.

'Not going.'

Sure enough, he was wearing jeans and his leather jacket rather than his uniform.

'Any reason or . . . ?'

'Emergency.'

Now that he'd caught up with me, I saw that he was even paler than I was, and had a rather attractive ruffled and unbrushed look.

'What's wrong?'

'One of the times I could do with that phone,' he said, panting. 'It's Christabel. She's found out.'

'What?' I was suddenly equally breathless.

'Fay just happened to visit yesterday, while we were at Fergus's, and she just happened to mention that you and I had been to the gallery, asking questions.'

'So what did your mother say?'

'It's not so much what she's saying, as how she's saying it. She pounced on me when I got home—'

'That makes two of us.'

'What?'

'Sorry, go on . . .'

'– and she accused me of spying and plotting with—' Andy halted, a flush on his white face.

'It's OK. I can guess. Fay told her I'm Natasha's daughter.'

'I'm afraid so. That made me so angry I told her we'd seen Fergus and what he'd said about her. Her and Fay.' Andy sat down and leaned against the birch tree.

'You told her! So what happened to masterly inactivity?'

'I know, I know, I just got carried away.'

'So what happened then?' I was hopping up and down with misery and impatience. How could Andy sit there in the sunshine? For God's sake, he was actually taking out his fags! 'Andy, how the hell can you *smoke* at a time like this?'

'Sorry, Rosa, but this is the sort of time when one *does* smoke.'

Then I saw that his hands were shaking, so I sat down as close as I dared and said, 'So is your mother upset rather than angry?'

'Got it in one. She began to, well, wail, I suppose, and said it wasn't her fault that your mother left the college, it was your mother's decision, and I wasn't to believe everything Fergus said because he'd been, quote, "besotted with Natasha".'

I looked away through the trees. Now that the leaves were falling, I could see the abandoned mill in the valley, and the heaps of junked cars.

'And then she ran up to her room and locked herself in. She didn't come down for supper, or breakfast, so this morning I left some coffee outside her door, but before I got back to the kitchen there was this crash, and she'd thrown the whole tray over the banisters.'

'It's all my fault,' I said, inclined to begin wailing myself, 'but I meant well, you know that, really I did!'

'Oh, Rosa, don't you start,' said Andy, in what I realized,

to my surprise, was a bored rather than an angry tone. 'I've had it to here with hysterical females.'

'Well, excuse me, but I'm not the one who's having to smoke to calm my shattered nerves.' And, meanly, I looked at Andy's hands, which were still trembling. 'And *I* didn't say a word to my mum. You could just've denied everything to Christabel. You didn't have to tell her we'd spoken to Fergus.'

To my relief, Andy actually laughed and stubbed out his cigarette, burying it among the crumpled leaves. 'OK, gypsy spitfire, don't let's fight, we're in—' He broke off, staring past me up the hill. 'Oh, Jesus.'

I'd been wondering if being a spitfire was a good thing, but now I followed his gaze and saw, through a gap in the trees, a figure speeding down Burnshead.

'But I thought she never went out?'

'She doesn't.' Andy got to his feet and I scrambled up after him.

Christabel, unmistakable in her long skirt, hair streaming behind her, a shawl flung round her shoulders, passed out of sight behind the Mowats' house and reappeared next to Kirsty's. She was walking swiftly, almost running.

'Where's she going?'

'Has your mother left yet?'

'But I told you, Mum doesn't know!' I really did wail. 'She doesn't know I've seen Fergus.'

'She won't be in ignorance much longer.'

Christabel appeared again between one red box and the next, her purple shawl picking up the colour of the

Michaelmas daisies in Kirsty's garden. In a couple of minutes she'd be at the end of the row.

I took off up the hillside, Andy behind me. I raced along the line of back gardens, kicked open the gate and was only delayed by the back door being locked. As I struggled with my keys, I heard the front doorbell chime.

'Oh no!' As I rushed into the kitchen, I heard Mum going down the hall. Her bag lay on the table. Another couple of minutes and she'd have been safely on her way to a round of contented hairdressing. But instead, as Andy and I followed her, she was opening the front door.

In the trusting manner of the country dweller she now claimed to be, Mum flung it wide open, letting in a flood of sunlight and cold fresh air.

Then, dazzled, caught off guard, she said, 'Yes, can I help you?' but Christabel, clutching at her shawl with both hands, said nothing.

CHAPTER twenty-five

I whooshed down the hall to Mum's side. She was now staring so hard at her unexpected visitor that she seemed completely unaware of my presence, far less that of Andy. The two women stood on either side of the threshold, Christabel even more unkempt than on our previous meeting, her lovely hair barely brushed, while Mum was all dressed up for her day's work. Yet what struck me was how *alike* they were. Mum's red hair fell down over her shoulders, as did Christabel's silvering locks; Mum's skirt was as long, and she wore a little embroidered jacket, the edges of which she now clutched together, imitating Christabel's gesture.

There was a long, long silence, during which I waited for either Christabel or Mum to do something dramatic.

However, what eventually happened was that Christabel said, in an only slightly husky voice, 'Natasha, I'd have known you anywhere. Forgive me for disturbing you, but I've only just discovered that we're neighbours.'

'Are we? I had no idea.' Mum was smaller than

Christabel, so she was standing very straight, head tilted back. 'This is quite a surprise, Christabel.' She didn't say that her old colleague was unchanged.

'We live just over the hill, we – that is, my son, Andy, and I.'

Mum turned at her gesture and saw Andy behind me. She looked from him to Christabel and back again. 'I thought he looked familiar, but I couldn't place the likeness.' She seemed annoyed with herself for not having made the connection. Then, and only then, did she look at me.

'I knew, Mum,' I said miserably. 'I knew you'd been at art college together.'

'When I saw the cards,' said Christabel, 'then I knew there must be some link.'

'Cards?' Mum's voice was harsh.

'Your tarot cards,' I said. 'I know you hid them, but I found them again and I showed them to Mrs Byron because Andy said she was interested in the tarot. I was just curious, I didn't mean any harm—'

'After all I said to you about meddling!' Mum turned away as though she could hardly bear to look at me. 'So you've taken up the black arts, Christabel? That's a big surprise, considering what you used to say about them.'

Christabel looked down. 'You're right to be angry, Natasha. I've said a lot of things for which I'm sorry and I've come to apologize. I – Fay and I, we didn't mean – we didn't know things would go so far.'

Mum put out her hand as though to silence Christabel and protect me.

'It's OK, Mum,' I said. 'I know everything that happened. I've spoken to Fergus.'

'Fergus!' Mum swung towards me, and for a moment her face seemed sharpened, the corners of her eyes, her nose, even her teeth. 'Is there no end to what you've been doing behind my back?'

But it was Andy she was looking at, and as I realized that she blamed him, just as Christabel had blamed me, I suddenly felt weary and cross, like a parent who's been dragging two kids round the supermarket.

'Yes, Andy and I went to see Fergus,' I said, 'and it was all my idea. I just wanted to know what all the fuss was about, and now that I do know, I just *don't care*. It was too long ago.'

And as I spoke, I knew it was true. No matter how vain and silly Mum had been, I'd been as bad, and no matter how wrongly Christabel might have acted, she regretted it now.

Mum was still staring at me. Her face had regained its old contours, but there was still an element of uncertainty to it, as though she could, at any moment, dissolve back into the creature I'd glimpsed.

It was Christabel, however, who spoke.

'Rosa's right,' she said. 'It was long ago, but you never intended to hurt anyone, Natasha, and I did. It started out as a bit of mischief. I never thought the papers would take it up as they did – I've regretted it ever since. Please forgive me, Natasha.'

And Christabel began to cry, but as elegantly as she did

everything else. Huge tears spilled out of her eyes and flowed down her cheeks. Weeping, I thought, rather than common crying.

Andy, though, was unimpressed.

'Honestly, Mother,' he said. It was the first time I'd heard him call her that. 'You're embarrassing everyone.'

Christabel dabbed at her eyes with her shawl, and Mum, horrified as usual by any display of emotion, said, 'Oh, Christabel, there's no need for you to carry on after all this time.'

I felt even tireder and crosser. I'd gone to all this trouble to uncover the truth, and nothing had changed! There was Mum being *nice* about Christabel's treachery, just as she'd been *nice* about my being rude to Grannie. It made me want to scream.

Christabel may have felt the same because she said, more sharply, 'I felt so guilty when you just disappeared. I heard you'd gone to Glasgow School of Art. Did you finish your course there?'

Mum gave a little laugh. 'No, no, I didn't. And just as well: I'm no loss to the art world.' She'd put her hand into her pocket, and now she drew it out, little points of silver showing between her clenched fingers. Her action was so unexpected that Christabel stepped back, but Mum simply shook out her car keys and said, 'But you'll excuse me, Christabel, I have to get on.' Then she turned to me. 'Rosaleen, you should be at school by now. I can't give you a lift – I'm going the wrong way. You can lock up behind me and catch the very next bus. I'll let the secretary know you're going to be late. Now where's my bag?'

Without waiting for an answer, she was down the tiny hall in two steps; she reappeared with her bag of hairdressing stuff, and was brushing past Christabel as though the poor woman had been transformed into a garden statue. A stone nymph, say, or a mournful shepherdess.

Christabel, however, still tear-stained, took a step after Mum, who was now opening the garage doors.

'But won't you forgive me?'

Mum paused in the act of throwing her bag into the boot beside her hair dryer. I wondered if she minded Christabel seeing these tools of her trade. At any rate she slammed down the lid and said, sounding exactly like Grannie, 'Christabel, the neighbours are looking at you!'

And sure enough, an elderly woman, a young mum and at least two children were peeping out of various windows.

Christabel paid no attention. 'Please, Natasha. I'm so sorry for what happened. Forgive me.'

It was only then that I realized, with a little bit of pleasure, that Mum hadn't actually accepted Christabel's apology. She wasn't being so nice after all. Now, wearing what I recognized as her peace-at-any-price expression, she finally said, 'Of course I do. Now I mustn't be any later for work. Rosa, shut the doors after me, please.'

And she got into the car, reversed into the road and drove off, keeping to just under the speed limit.

CHAPTER twenty-six

We stood there like stookies, all equally taken aback by Mum's rapid departure. I moved first. I trotted obediently over to the garage doors and closed them. Christabel was finally drying her eyes properly, using, instead of her shawl, a proper linen hankie which she'd had tucked up her sleeve. As I watched her, I realized that was exactly what Mum did. She despised tissues and had a collection of wee lace hankies which she actually kept folded up in lavender, as a nice old lady would.

'I must be getting back.' Christabel was beginning to look around, presumably surprised to find herself so far from home. 'I do apologize, Rosa. I hope I haven't made your mother late. Come along, Andy, we mustn't delay Rosa any longer.'

Andy stepped forwards. 'But aren't you on your way to the shops? I'll come with you.'

He looked hard at me. Of course, Christabel's agora-phobia was the one thing I still wasn't supposed to know about.

'Oh no, not just now, I've no money with me, nothing. I just rushed out to have a word with Natasha.' Christabel turned back towards the hill, pulling her shawl round her shoulders. She wasn't dressed nearly warmly enough for the bright, chilly morning.

Then I saw the look on Andy's face. Resigned, angry and – the emotion most recently aroused in me by my mother – just plain fed up. I mean, there was Mum, behaving as though Christabel's appearance were simply an annoying obstacle to getting to work, and now Christabel was heading for her house without taking advantage of her valour in leaving it.

'Why don't you come in for a cup of coffee?' I said. 'I'm so late another half hour won't make any difference. Do come in. Please. We've got some Bei and Nannini.'

At the mention of the upmarket brand, Christabel actually wavered. Perhaps she was remembering her own breakfast, smashed on the stone floor. I held the door open with what I hoped was a winning smile, while Andy gripped her elbow and almost pushed her over the threshold. As he did so, we exchanged glances, a pair of adults humouring a difficult child.

I ushered them into the sitting room, and had the pleasure of seeing Christabel look with approval at Mum's tawny walls and patterned throws.

'What a lovely room,' she said. 'Natasha always had such an eye.'

I wondered when Christabel had last been in any room outside Drumglass.

'Do sit down,' I said. 'I'll make the coffee.'

I hurried through to the kitchen, and, as I was putting on the kettle, Andy put his head round the door. 'I don't suppose there's any more of that killer cake?'

'For breakfast?'

'Lunch, tea, dinner.'

'I'll look.'

'Thanks, Rosa.' I knew he didn't mean just the cake. 'I'd better go back and keep an eye on her. In case she makes a dash for it.'

I set a tray with some lovely wee cups and saucers – white, painted with blue flowers – which Mum had found in a car boot sale, and a cafetière of extra-strong coffee. Luckily for Andy there was also a lemon sponge cake.

The next few minutes were spent in the usual pouring and passing stuff, while I wondered which would be worse: ignoring the scene that had just occurred, or discussing it in detail.

Christabel, however, had recovered at the first sip of coffee, and was displaying the same sort of good manners as Andy sometimes did. She praised the coffee, Mum's décor and the china, which particularly impressed her. 'May Queen,' she said. 'So pretty. Quite rare nowadays.'

'Mum picked it up in a sale somewhere.'

'She always had lovely things.'

'Really?'

'Oh yes, her clothes, the things in her room. She had such a knack of putting things together.'

This was a completely new picture – Christabel visiting Mum. I'd got the impression they were sworn enemies.

'Yes,' she continued. She had the dreamy look which Dad wore when remembering *his* student days. 'Fergus lived in Keir Street, right next to the Flodden Wall – you could see the castle from his window – and when your mother moved in with him, she made it so pretty, not a bit like a student flat. We all used to go round there and listen to Fergus play and Natasha would read the— All the men were crazy about her. Not just Sean. I dare say we girls were jealous. And we all fancied Fergus. That's how the rumours started.' She halted, her dream fading. 'But that was no excuse.' Then, abruptly, she shook herself back into being a polite visitor. 'And which subjects are you studying, Rosa? Do you do art?'

Eventually, after I'd answered all Christabel's questions about my academic choices and explained that Dad was a teacher, but not at my school, she rose to her feet.

'Thank you so much, Rosa, that was delicious. Are you coming, Andy? You ought to be on your way to school.'

'I'll nip back for my stuff, then I'll be off.'

He looked at me behind Christabel's back, raising his eyebrows.

I shook my head slightly. 'Me too. Mum phoned the school, so the secretary will be on the lookout.'

He smiled. 'I'll see you on the bus tonight then. The *late* bus.'

Christabel, who had reached the front door, looked back at us.

'Awright, big man,' I said, in my broadest accent.

Andy grinned at me and, as I passed him to open the door, he reached out and squeezed my hand.

When I eventually arrived at school, it was the middle of break, so I went to the office to check in.

The secretary, renowned for her sharp suits and fashion-statement glasses, gave me a very odd look.

'Is everything all right at home, Rosa? This is the third time this week you've been absent. Your mother said it was a family emergency.'

All we needed now was someone from the social services landed on the doorstep.

'Everything's fine now, thank you,' I said. 'I won't be off again.'

There wasn't much she could say to this, so after a bit of tsking and peering at me through the retro specs she marked me in, and I went to find Clary.

'Where on earth have you been?' she demanded. She was leaning against the wall outside the music room, eating a squashed fruit health bar, a typical Clary snack. With her shiny loose hair and glowing skin she looked as though she should be strolling through an alpine meadow rather than loitering in our dingy corridor. And there was still something odd about her that I couldn't identify.

'And where were you yesterday?' she continued. 'I looked for you everywhere.'

'I'm sorry. I bunked off, but Mum caught me out, so I'm going to have to watch it from now on.'

'So where did you get to? We thought you might want to come to this great old gangster film.'

'So which *we* is this?' I was becoming more and more confused. I'd never seen Clary blushing about her movie habit, as she was now.

'Oh, that friend Andy mentioned – my old neighbour Ben.'

'Who?'

'Yes, remember, I asked Andy to give Ben's sister my number, so they invited me round on Sunday—'

'But you said you were with your grandparents!'

'That was for lunch, so after lunch I went round. Of course, I had homework but Ben said, bring it with me—'

'A study date!' I exclaimed.

Why had I ever doubted Clary? Her old angelic halo was gleaming around her again. It was *Ben's* messages for which she had been checking her mobile!

'It was no such thing!' said Clary. 'Stephanie was there, and some of her friends, and, when we'd finished our work, we had a bonfire in their back garden, because that's what we used to do when we were little kids.'

This was so much the sort of innocent thing that Clary would do on a date that I burst out laughing.

'Ben and Clary up a tree, K-i-s-s-i-n-g!'

I felt incredibly light-hearted and happy. It didn't matter that Mum still had to be properly angry with me, or that she and Christabel weren't going to fall into one another's arms on a wave of forgiveness and unconditional love.

It was Ben whom Clary fancied!

'So how come you didn't tell me all this on Monday?' I said.

Clary's face was now light geranium, which is the reddest and hottest she ever goes. 'There wasn't anything to tell,' she said. 'I mean, I really liked Ben when we were kids but, as I said, we lost touch when they moved. And I knew you'd laugh about the bonfire.'

'*Anyone* would laugh about that! So what did you do yesterday?'

'Ben texted me to ask if I wanted to go to a film, so I went to look for you because a friend of his was going as well—'

'First a study date, now a double date at the movies!'

I could hardly believe this was serious Clary speaking, and obviously she couldn't either, because she went pinker as she said, 'So Marisa came instead – she's really nice when you get her away from Leanne—'

'Did you sit in the back row?'

'Certainly not! This was a *serious* classic film in *French*.'

Only Clary would go with a boy to see a subtitled movie.

'Anyway,' she continued, before I could start laughing again, 'where did you get to?'

'I was meeting Andy, although *not* in a dark cinema, we—'

The bell rang.

'Tell me later!' cried Clary, and she waltzed away, gracefully skirting Debs and Franklin, who were saying a fervent temporary farewell at the next corner.

I watched her go, as earlier that morning I'd watched Andy and Christabel climbing the hill back to Drumglass.

Stranger things have happened. If Christabel could appear on the doorstep, then Clary could have boyfriend. *I* could have a boyfriend.

And then I thought about Fergus, alone in his dark basement, and Mum, zapping from one haircut to the next, and how they'd once been this golden couple, and now Fergus was forgotten and Mum had never got to be a great painter, and—

'So what's got into *her*?' Debs, catching up with me, rolled her eyes suggestively in the direction of the disappearing Clary. 'You'd almost think she'd found someone brainy enough to be her boyfriend.'

'Stranger things've happened,' I said.

CHAPTER twenty-seven

'Mum,' I said. 'Mum, weren't you surprised when Mrs Byron – Christabel – showed up this morning?'

I'd been trying to get Mum on her own for hours, but after supper she'd taken her coffee through to the sitting room to watch some TV programme with Dad, and then she'd wrenched Nairn away from his beloved computer, insisting that he help with the washing-up.

'Your sister's been working her fingers to the bone since we came here, while I haven't seen you get your wee paws dirty once! No male skivers in my house!'

The only sign she gave that something earth-shattering had happened was when she accused Nairn of polishing off an entire cake.

'That wasn't Nairn,' I'd said quickly. 'Andy ate it. I asked him and his mother in for coffee after you'd left.'

Then the oddest look had passed over her face, and when Nairn started his 'Rosa's got a boyfriend' chant, she'd all but boxed his ears.

Anyway, I'd finally run her to earth by creeping

downstairs last thing at night, after I'd heard Dad go to bed. She was in the kitchen, making herself a cup of camomile tea.

'Rosa, I thought you were in bed! Don't sneak up on me like that!'

Mum whirled round, steadying herself with one hand on the worktop. She looked tired, in the way that redheads do – pale but pink-nosed. It would've been easier just to have gone back to bed, but I couldn't bear the way she was ignoring Christabel's visit and my having seen Fergus. I'd said that what had happened in the past didn't matter to me, but did it truly not matter to her?

'Sorry,' I said. 'I thought you'd heard me.'

'How can I hear you if you creep about the place like a spy?'

I sat down at the table. 'Mum, I'm sorry I interfered, but I just wanted to know—'

'It was none of your business! How could you go and speak to Fergus – and Christabel?'

'I've never spoken to her. I mean, I've only met her once before—'

'And if you know so much now, madam, you could've given me warning she was living nearby. I was bound to have run into her at the shops—'

'No, you wouldn't,' I said. 'She's got agoraphobia. She never goes out. Today was the first time in ages.'

'Oh.' Mum sat down opposite me. 'Is that true?'

'Of course it's true. Andy does all the shopping, and Fay brings her embroidery thread and stuff. She makes things for Fay's gallery.'

Madeeha younis madeeha younis Madeeha younis
Madeeha younis madeeha younis madeeha younis
madeeha younis madaeha younis madeeha younis
mad33ha younis

'Och, Fay,' said Mum, exactly as Fergus had done. This news about Christabel had brought her up short. 'Christabel was always the nervous type, so I don't suppose it's any surprise really. But she was so pretty: she was the pretty one and Fay was the clever one – you know how friendships go. So that's how things have ended up?'

'Yes. Christabel and Andy's father are divorced, and Christabel and Andy live in this sort of tumbledown house just over the hill. Christabel can't go out to work, so I don't think they've got much money.'

'That must be bit of a comedown for Christabel.' Mum looked almost happy as she said this, and I was glad that she could be plain nasty for once.

'So you didn't exactly like her?'

'Of course I didn't like her! Her and that Fay, toffee-nosed boarding-school girls.'

'But Christabel said she used to come round to your flat—'

'She came round all right, but it was to make eyes at Fergus.'

I could picture the scene. The smoky, candle-lit room; Fergus, dangerously dark and handsome, bent over his guitar; and Christabel, posed in the window against the out-line of the castle – no wonder Mum had been mad at my asking her in for coffee.

'Still and all, I'm sorry if things haven't worked out for her.' Mum had swiftly returned to her usual kindly self. She got up and fetched her tea.

'Mum,' I said cautiously, 'I *am* sorry, really. It's just – once

Christabel told me you'd been to college together, I don't know – yes, I do: it's because Dad *lied*. I asked him, and he said you'd never been to college. So then I had to find out the truth.'

Mum sat down again. 'I'm sorry your father didn't tell you, but he knows I hate to speak about it.'

'But you didn't do anything wrong!'

It felt strange to be sitting up with Mum in the sleeping house. She was wearing her old pink silk kimono, which usually made her look so pretty, but tonight the colour heightened the red around her eyes and turned her freckles into blotches.

'Why didn't you tell me? If I'd known, then I'd never have gone ferreting around.'

'It's all so long ago! And as you said yourself, it doesn't matter any more.'

'But it must matter to you and Christabel,' I said, 'or why would you both be so upset? And what about the boy who died? It must still matter to his family.'

'Poor Sean.' Mum had been fiddling with her cup of tea, but now her hands fell limply onto the table. 'That was a terrible thing I did, reading his cards. I'll never forgive myself.' She shook her head, and then sat staring down into her tea, as though it were a deep well.

I spoke in a whisper. 'Did you *know* he was going to die?'

'No. But . . . I wasn't surprised when I heard. I'd just been playing before, but now it seemed as though – as though—'

'You could do it for real,' I finished.

'Yes.' Mum looked at me. 'Oh, Rosa, you haven't been reading the cards, have you?'

I nodded. 'But I won't be doing it again. I gave them to Fergus, so's I wouldn't be tempted.'

'Fergus warned me. And then when all the trouble started, he wanted me to stay and brazen it out – but I couldn't do it. And do you know why, Rosa?' Mum raised her head. 'Because I deserved every word of those rumours, every word in those newspaper stories. I may not have *caused* Sean to die, but I'd meddled with his fate, and made things worse for his poor parents.'

'So you punished yourself by running away?'

'Yes, that's what I did.'

'But what about Fergus? Didn't you love him?' If young Fergus had been my boyfriend, could I have left him?

'You've met him. What do you think?'

I didn't say anything, and for a moment Mum didn't either.

'He'd have broken my heart in the end,' she said finally. 'We all knew he'd be a star some day, and then he'd be on the road, girls throwing themselves at him, and he liked a drink, even then . . .'

When she didn't go on, I said, 'So it was easier to leave first?'

'It wasn't *easy*, but – och, it was everything: Fergus, Sean, the papers. And the other thing was' – Mum gave what I realized was a hysterical laugh – 'when you got down to it, I wasn't all that good at art.'

'What do you mean?'

'I was so delighted when I got into the college, and Grannie and Grandad were that proud, but when I saw other people's work, I realized I'd never be a painter.'

'But, Mum, you're brilliant at interior dec and stuff! Christabel said you always were!'

'I could've changed courses, but after everything that had happened it just didn't seem worthwhile any more.'

'So you went away and became a hairdresser?' I said flatly.

'And what's wrong with that?' said Mum, sounding more like her old self. 'Having their hair nice makes people happy. And if I hadn't gone to Glasgow, I'd never have met your father.'

That was what I'd been thinking ever since I'd met Fergus. What a difference the fall of one card had made!

Mum took a sip of her tea. 'Stone cold,' she said, putting down the cup. 'Now that's enough talk. Time for bed.'

The spell was breaking. We were tilting back into ordinary old family life again.

'Do you mind that I gave Fergus the cards?' I said quickly, before she could get up. 'It was the little embroidered bag he liked – he remembered you making it.'

'Ach, the old rogue,' she said. All through our conversation, her face had been changing, different colours and feelings, and even ages, crossing it. And now, all at once, it was beautiful again. Then she did get up, turning her back to me. 'How was he? Was he drinking?'

'Not noticeably.' I decided that whisky in your tea didn't count. 'Did you know that song "Red Bird" was about you?'

'Of course I knew! Although, typical Fergus, it came years too late. And if you ever took the time to listen to his music, you'd see that half the songs are about his women – Lizzie o' Leith, Debra in Nebraska, "On the Road With Beatrice Jones" – there's no end to them. Us.'

'But you sing it.'

Mum was still turned away so that I couldn't see her face. 'It's still nice to have your own song when all's said and done.'

Nice! I just hate that word!

'And what about Dad? Does he know?'

'Your father and I agreed long ago not to discuss the past.' Mum spoke sharply. 'Of course he knows about Sean, and that I went out with Fergus, but that doesn't stop him enjoying his music.'

'Very nice of him,' I said, but Mum didn't pick up on my sarcasm.

'Yes, that's your father all over.' She sounded as though she were smiling.

'So everybody ended up just fine. Except for Sean.'

'Yes, except for poor Sean.' Mum tipped her tea down the sink and rinsed the cup. Then she finally turned back to face me. 'Now, Rosa, you be careful with that Andy Byron.'

I sighed dramatically. 'I know he's Christabel's son and all, but he's just a *friend*. We'd never have been trailing around town together if we hadn't been looking for Fergus.' Then I had a brainwave. 'Actually, I think he might fancy Clary.'

'Clary?' I could see Mum turning it over in her head and

seeing the suitability, as I'd done before I knew about Ben, wonderful Ben.

I crossed my fingers under the table. 'I don't know for sure, of course, but Clary's started to wear her hair loose.'

As I'd guessed it would, news of a hairstyle change clinched Mum's suspicion.

'I just hope she's too sensible to get carried away.'

'I'm sure she is,' I said solemnly. 'You know Clary.'

'It really is time for bed.' Mum began to bustle round the kitchen, checking switches and locks. Then she paused. 'And this conversation is just between ourselves.'

There was nothing I could say except, 'OK, Mum,' but I crossed my fingers again. I couldn't not tell Andy.

'Now off to bed with you.'

I rose to my feet, and Mum gave me the wee kiss that was the closest the McBride family came to a hug.

'Night-night then.'

'Night,' I replied, and trailed up to bed, leaving Mum setting the table for breakfast.

However, as I snuggled down under my patchwork quilt, I felt twitchy and dissatisfied. Mum had been punished for reading the cards, but she had something to remember. She could look back and see herself surrounded by admirers, and loved by a man who would write her a song.

I wriggled around a bit more. And then I knew what was wrong with me. I was jealous.

CHAPTER twenty-eight

'Are you totally positive your mother never comes up here?'

'Positive. Man of the house has to have his privacy. It's the pay-off for actually being the man of the house.'

'OK.'

I looked uncertainly around Andy's bedroom. I didn't quite know if it was for better or worse that Christabel wouldn't appear on the threshold.

'Is she all right?' I said.

'More or less.'

It was the Saturday following the dramatic mid-week events, and Andy and I had sneaked up to his room, being careful to avoid Christabel. I remembered him saying that he didn't bring people back home, so as we'd climbed the spiral staircase, I'd wondered if I were the first girl to follow him to his turret.

'This is so amazing,' I said, still looking around the room, which was a very peculiar shape, like one of the pieces in my patchwork quilt. 'If only you were a girl, you could let your hair down out of the window, like Rapunzel.'

'Wasted on a bloke then?'

'Oh yeah.' I wandered over to the small square window and looked out. It was a miserable, dreich afternoon, and far below I could see Christabel, once more digging in the rain, and beyond her the blue Pentland hills. I understood, all over again, why Andy loved Drumglass. I would too, if it had been mine.

I sighed and turned back into the room, where Andy was guddling about in the fireplace.

'You're not lighting a real fire, are you?'

We'd had a fireplace in our old flat, but only an actual fire on special occasions.

'Of course. You mean there's some other way of getting warm?'

'You do have electricity, don't you?'

'Yes, but the wiring won't take a fire.'

'For some reason I believe you.'

'Anyway, this is for you. I don't always bother.'

'I'm honoured.' And although I said it ironically, I really meant it. Ever since we arrived at Burnshead, Andy seemed to be the only person who cared if I were cold or wet or unhappy.

'Go on, take your coat off, make yourself at home.'

I took off my jacket and sat down on the floor beside Andy, who was arranging logs on the fire as skilfully as one of Nairn's Native Americans.

'Do you want some coffee?'

'Don't tell me you're going to boil a kettle on the old camp fire?'

'I don't go that far. I've got an electric kettle.'

'I thought you said the wiring—'

'I take my life in my hands every time I use it.'

'Go on then.'

While Andy made us mugs of coffee – which, unlike Christabel's, was cheapest instant, black, with loads of sugar – I leaned back against a big, tatty armchair. Unsurprisingly, Andy's room was unlike any other lads' I'd ever seen. One, it was fairly tidy; two, there was no TV; and three, there were no posters of football stars or bands or busty celebrities. What he did have, pinned over the bed, were several photos, torn from magazines, of gloomy foreign cities. Prague in the snow. Venice in the rain. There was also a big carved chest of drawers, a couple of shelves of books, and on the floor an absolutely gorgeous carpet in a deep, faded red, with a little blue pattern hopscotching over it.

'This was my father's room when he was a kid,' said Andy, handing me my coffee. 'He liked it for the same reason I do. It's miles away from the rest of the house.'

I hid a tiny, excited shiver by playing with the buttons on my new angora top. Yesterday afternoon Clary, amazingly for her, had announced that she wanted to go clothes shopping, so while she bought a ruffly off-the-shoulder number, I'd got this clingy thing which fitted better than my usual clothes, but was less revealing than my black silk. According to the label, it was a colour called Clove Carnation.

'Weren't you scared when you were little?' I said, in case I'd been silent for too long.

'Ghosts?'

Then we were both quiet for a moment as Andy came and sat beside me. 'Sorry, Rosa,' he said. 'No ghosts.'

I thought about Sean, and wondered if he'd had brothers and sisters, and, if he had, whether they still remembered him.

Andy, as though he'd followed my thoughts, said, 'Is your brother better?'

I sighed. 'Yes. He's going back to school next week.'

Mum's wish that the past should lie undisturbed had not been fulfilled. Nairn had sensed that she was upset, and had his worst asthma attack yet, out of sympathy. In the kerfuffle following this, Mum had told Dad about my exploits, and he'd been absolutely furious, because I was the one who'd upset her. However, when I'd reminded him that he always said truth was sacred, he'd looked terribly sad and then gone into his room and put on some heartbreaking fiddle music.

Then, of course, I'd felt awful, and Nairn, who'd been given an edited version of events, began to snuffle again, and Grannie, who'd come to look after him, had her turn being angry with me. I might as well have been one of those witchcraft dolls, stuck full of pins of other people's bad temper and hurt feelings.

Grannie, however, also gave the impression that she'd been longing to speak about Sean and Fergus – especially Fergus – for years, and now that the ban was lifted she cornered me whenever she got the chance and went on and on about how the evil folk singer had led her wee lass astray; how the papers had then savaged her; and how the sly posh girls had ganged up on her, until I absolutely understood why Mum had preferred silence.

Andy leaned back beside me. 'Are your family speaking to you yet?'

'Yes and no. Mum's gone back to pretending everything's just fine, Nairn's being extra nice, Grannie won't shut up and Dad's not speaking to anyone much.' I slumped back against the chair. 'Come to think of it, business as usual.'

Andy put his arm round me. 'C'mon, Rosa, it can't be so bad. Fergus was pleased to see you – more than pleased, I'd say – and surely it's better for your family to have things out in the open.'

'But I thought everything would be *better*!'

'That's so like you: you just want everybody to be happy and contented.'

That was what Mum tried to do. I sat up straight.

'I do not! I just wanted everyone to be honest – there's nothing wrong with that.'

'So have you told your mother about the fair yet?'

'Not in detail. But I will.' I could feel myself growing hot, and not just from the fire.

Andy put his hand out. 'Come back, Rosa. Don't mind me, I'm just naturally mean.'

'No, you're not.' I fitted myself into the curve of his arm.

'Oh yes, I am. You just don't know me well enough.'

I thought that if he were mean it would hardly be surprising, given his weird background.

'So has Christabel calmed down? Any more broken cups?'

'Not cups.' Andy rubbed his free hand over his face as though he could wipe away the creases around his eyes. 'But I can report progress. I phoned my father this morning.'

'But I thought you said you hadn't a phone,' I said irrelevantly, too surprised to say anything more sensible.

'There are still such things as phone boxes.'

'So what did you say?'

'I told him Christabel was a lot worse, so he huffed for a bit and then he said he'd get in touch with an old school-friend who's a psychiatrist and ask him to come and see her. She shouldn't be able to fool an expert.'

'But won't she be furious with you, like she was over the GP?'

'Probably. But what I'm hoping is that she's so miserable, she'll admit she needs help. I mean, she could pretend before that everything was great, but after that scene with your mother, she can hardly claim to be normal. Standing in your front garden crying, with half the neighbourhood looking on! And she's been extra nervous ever since.'

'Oh don't say that, it just makes me feel worse!'

'But don't you see, it's a good thing in the end. Dad wouldn't be sending his friend to the rescue if he wasn't worried about Christabel's behaviour becoming, well, embarrassing. It would never do for the noble name of Byron to be sullied by . . . by . . .'

'Public eccentricity?'

'Yeah, crying in gardens.'

'Well, I think crying in gardens is a lot better than not speaking about something for twenty years, like Mum. There ought to be more of it, crying, stamping, shouting, the lot.'

'Going to be a psychiatrist, are you?' Andy gave me his most infuriating grin.

I sat up again. 'And why shouldn't I? There's nothing to stop me.' I'd spoken without thinking, but as I heard my words I realized they were true. I could do it if I wanted. It would be like reading the tarot, but without the magic. I could make things better instead of worse. It certainly wasn't something to be sneered at, as Andy was still doing.

'You'd have to wear a suit. And glasses. I can just see you. Dr McBride!' He laughed out loud, and I realized, with a small, unhappy shock, that this was something he hardly ever did. 'And you couldn't wear these fancy clip things in your hair – no one would take you seriously.' He removed one of the clips, and I snatched it back.

'They would too.' I repinned my hair, which I'd spent ages arranging in front of my mirror. 'Anyway, what are you going to do that's so serious and special?'

'I know what I'm going to do now.' And before I had time to prepare myself for the thing I'd been longing for, Andy kissed me.

Immediately, the chair against which we were both leaning scooted backwards, and so, much sooner than I'd expected, I found myself lying on the floor, but Andy chivalrously reached down a cushion and put it under my head. Then he began to kiss me in ways which were indeed serious and special, and I kissed him back, while dozens of contradictory messages bopped around in my head. Perhaps I wasn't doing it well enough, and he'd realize how inexperienced I was, or perhaps I was leading him on, and we ought to stop before it was too late, or perhaps I ought to be remembering all the things our guidance teacher had said about teenage relationships and responsibility, but the loudest voice was saying that this was the most blissful and exciting thing that had ever happened to me, and that I was going to enjoy it, because whatever happened in the future, I'd always have this, kissing Andy by the fire, just as Mum had the memory of Fergus.

'Rosa, we ought to stop.' Andy sat up.

'What?' I said dizzily. He'd moved away from me, leaving my body lonely and discomfited. I must've been doing it wrong.

'Oh, Rosa.'

'You're always saying that – "Oh, Rosa." What do you mean?'

'I just mean we ought to stop.'

'But I don't want to – stop, that is.'

'Do you think I do? Look, Rosa, we're friends, aren't we?'

'So? Don't you – don't you . . . kiss girls you're friends with?'

He didn't look at me. 'Sometimes I do. And sometimes I kiss girls I don't even like very much.'

'Are you saying you like me too much to kiss me?' I sat up and faced him. My body was doing all sorts of complicated things, and my clothes felt much too tight. 'What sort of an excuse is that?'

'Of course it's not an excuse!' He sounded genuinely angry. 'The thing is, I won't be around for much longer. Whether or not Christabel gets better, I'm going to take off.'

'What?' I cooled down from hot to freezing in half a second.

'I told you I'd been thinking about it. Look, the longer I stay here, the more dependent Christabel becomes on me. If I don't get out soon, I'll be here for ever.'

'But where will you go?' I looked across the room at his travel pictures, only now understanding their significance.

'I always fancied Prague. Or Berlin. Somewhere gloomy and cold with a lot of architecture. And cafés.'

'What about money?'

'Sleep on someone's floor, work in a bar, call in a few favours from Dad.'

I hoped I wasn't going to cry. Any dream I'd ever allowed myself of Andy and I going to university together disappeared into the rain that was now beating against the turret window.

'That's not going to get you very far in the long run,' I said. 'What about exams and stuff?'

'There's no rule says you have to be educated.'

'I suppose.'

I shivered, and Andy moved further away from me to toss a couple of logs on the fire. It flared up, revealing the cosy reds and blues of the carpet.

'That's a lovely carpet,' I said, trying to keep my voice

steady. I ran one finger along the blue maze of the pattern. 'Is it magic?'

'No, unfortunately, or things would be very different around here. But it is Persian, a relic of the Byrons' former glory. It's hidden up here because Christabel's afraid Fay would get her mitts on it if she ever saw it.'

'Some friend.'

'Well, unless Christabel lets someone help her get better, she won't make any new ones.'

'That reminds me – Mum said, next time I saw you, to say that she's got loads of embroidery and sewing magazines in case Christabel ever wants to borrow them.'

'A peace offering?'

'As good as it gets.'

'There you go: before you know it, our mothers will be meeting up to swap patterns over their cappuccinos.'

'It's not like you to be so optimistic,' I said bitterly.

With every sentence we were returning to our old, bickering, boy-and-girl relationship.

'But,' I said, 'if that did happen, and she got better and made friends and stuff, you wouldn't have to go.'

'Oh yes, I would.' Andy stretched out his hand across what was now the quite wide space between us and ran his finger down the length of my woolly arm. 'Don't you see, Rosa, I have to go, so I can't make any – any sort of promise to you.'

'I'm not asking for your promises!'

'I know you're not, but I don't want to hurt anyone else.'

But you've hurt me already, I wanted to say. I've been waiting and waiting for you to kiss me, and now you say you're not going to do it again? Why do you think I've been doing my hair and wearing make-up, and why do you think I came here today, all tarted up in snazzy new clothes? And then I remembered what I'd just said about crying in gardens being better than silence, and I remembered how beautiful Mum looked when she thought about Fergus, so I said, 'You've got a very high opinion of yourself, Andy Byron, if you believe you're going to break my heart. And who do you think you are, making these high-handed decisions for both of us? Perhaps I'd rather have something to look back on, when you're stravaiging round eastern Europe, than just being your friend.'

For the second time that afternoon I'd made Andy laugh. 'I was right when I called you a gypsy spitfire,' he said, leaning against the precarious chair. It swooshed backwards again and he went with it.

'I wasn't being funny,' I said, upright and dignified.

'Neither was I. Being funny, I mean.' He was addressing the ceiling. 'But you're right. I was making up your mind for you.'

'That is so patronizing.'

'Oh, you look sooo fierce.' He lay on his back, grinning.

'I mean it,' I said. 'I'll take the risk.' And I lay down beside him on the allegedly unmagical carpet.

Andy propped himself up on one elbow, and for the first time we looked at one another properly and completely.

SASKIA'S JOURNEY
by Theresa Breslin

*Why does Saskia feel so disturbed when she
goes to spend a few weeks with her reclusive great-aunt
Alessandra up on the Scottish coast? Why does she feel
such a sense of menace around Alessandra's house
when she has never been there before.*

Just as the sea must give up its bounty, will
Alessandra reveal the secrets – and tragedies – of their
family's past? Somehow Saskia knows that she must
understand more if she is to find the direction she
needs for her future. For only then can she break the
cycle, find the courage to stand up for what
she wants – and be free . . .

'Themes of love and forgiveness are at the heart of this
haunting tale of self-discovery . . . truly memorable'
The Bookseller

'Delicately balanced narrative'
Scottish Sunday Herald

'A sensitive, finely structured novel'
Books for Keeps

0 552 54865 0

CORGI BOOKS

THE SISTERHOOD OF THE TRAVELLING PANTS

by Ann Brashares

Four best friends, one pair of jeans and a few important rules:

- You must never wash the Pants
- You must never double-cuff the Pants. It's tacky. There will never be a time when this will not be tacky.
- You must never say the word 'phat' while wearing the Pants. You must also never think 'I am fat' while wearing the Pants.
- You must not pick your nose while wearing the Pants. You may, however, scratch casually at your nostril while really kind of picking.
- You must write to your Sisters throughout the summer, no matter how much fun you are having without them.

Quirky, original and heart-warming, *The Sisterhood of the Travelling Pants* is an irresistible celebration of female friendship and self-discovery.

'An outstanding and vivid book that will stay with readers for a long time'   *Publishers Weekly*

0 552 54827 8

CORGI BOOKS

THE SECOND SUMMER
OF THE SISTERHOOD

by Ann Brashares

'This is it,' Carmen breathed. The moment was all around them. She remembered the vow from last summer. They all remembered it.

'To honour the Pants and the Sisterhood And this moment and this summer and the rest of our lives Together and apart.'

Spend a long, lush summer with four best friends as they share secrets – and swap a pair of truly magical jeans.

A *New York Times* bestseller – the sequel to *The Sisterhood of the Travelling Pants*

0 552 55050 7

CORGI BOOKS

RANI & SUKH

by Bali Rai

'Man, she's wicked like one of them Bollywood actresses . . .

Sikh reckons Rani is the most fanciable girl in school.
She's got just the kind of look he goes for . . .

Rani can't stop thinking about Sukh either.
Talk about fit. Beautiful amber-brown eyes, like pools
you could jump into . . .

But Rani is a Sandhu, and Sukh is a Bains – and
sometimes names can lead to terrible trouble . . .

*A powerful and gripping novel that sweeps the reader from
modern-day Britain to the Punjab in the 1960s and back
again in a ceaseless cycle of tragedy and conflict.*

0 552 54890 1

CORGI BOOKS